THE SOAP OPERA
SLAUGHTERS

THE SOAP OPERA SLAUGHTERS

MARVIN KAYE

PUBLISHED FOR THE CRIME CLUB BY
DOUBLEDAY & COMPANY, INC.
GARDEN CITY, NEW YORK
1982

Library of Congress Cataloging in Publication Data

Kaye, Marvin.
The soap opera slaughters.

I. Title.
PS3561.A866S6   1982   813'.54
ISBN 0-385-18361-5
Library of Congress Catalog Card Number 82–45530

First Edition

To two very special friends,
BEVERLY PENBERTHY and
LOUISE SHAFFER and
their alter egos,
PAT RANDOLPH and
RAE WOODARD;
and
in memory of
BOB ANDERSON and
BROOKE HAMILTON
(a/k/a STEPHANIE),
and the late MARY RYAN—
three alter egos that I really miss.

ACKNOWLEDGMENTS

Deepest thanks and affection to the ineffably lovely dedicatees, LOUISE SHAFFER (Rae Woodard on ABC-TV's "Ryan's Hope") and BEVERLY PENBERTHY (Pat Randolph on NBC-TV's "Another World"), for arranging for me to watch their shows at work. Special thanks to Louise for her witty advice and keen insight into the psychology of daytime drama actors and to Beverly for her marvelous ceiling-to-roof guided tour of the labyrinthine NBC Brooklyn studios. Most of all, I thank both *belles dames* for the precious gift of friendship.

I am grateful for the cooperation of the above shows and their executive staffs, including "Ryan's Hope" producer Ellen Barrett and her assistant Babs dePina (a fellow Wolfe Pack-er) and "Another World" producer Mary S. Bonner and her associates Holly Evarts and Kathy Chambers.

Special thanks to the guiding lights of Soap Opera Festivals Inc., Joyce Becker—with whose showmanship I am much impressed—and her gracious partner and husband, Allan Sugarman. Thanks, too, to Audrey Wertheim for making such smooth arrangements for me to attend a Becker-Sugarman festival . . . much more civilized than the event herein depicted.

The above persons gave generously of their time and knowledge. Any accidental or intentional errors or perversions of fact or probability are, of course, strictly my own.

Once more I thank my dear friend Dave Goldenberg for technical advice pertaining to pharmaceutical knavery, as well as those indispensable references, the Physicians' Desk Reference and Dr. James W. Long's *The Essential Guide to Prescription Drugs* (Harper & Row, 1977).

Lastly, the eternal admiration of a serial buff to Carleton E. Morse's pioneering "One Man's Family" and its latter-day spiritual stepchild, "Days of Our Lives," with its Hilary Quayle lookalikes, Deidre Hall and her charming sister, Andrea Hall Lovell.

—MARVIN KAYE
Manhattan, 1981

If I hadn't paused to watch the goldfish ripping up the *anarchis*, I would've missed the precommercial teaser on the Channel 14 newscast.

"—unidentified naked man plunges to a bloody death from the rooftop of a Manhattan TV studio. We'll have details after—"

It didn't mean anything to me then, though "naked" caught my attention, just the way the copywriter planned. Certainly I had no idea the coming report was the first link in a chain involving Hilary that I would have to unweld.

I was in a lousy mood. Loneliness is watching one comet and two fantails—Charlie, Jackie and Marty Goldfish—systematically defoliate the greenery in their ten-gallon aquarium tank at eleven o'clock at night. On a Saturday. In Philadelphia. The apartment was empty, The Old Man was busy wrecking his wheels in a midwestern demolition derby while I tried to salvage his flybitten detective agency, and the telephone remained silent. The latter being the chief irritant. Hilary had almost a week to call, but she didn't, not even after I squeezed an apology into the thirty seconds her recording machine allows.

Several months earlier, I'd been employed as secretary-houseboy-copywriter for Hilary's PR firm in her ground-floor West End Avenue apartment in Manhattan's mid-Eighties. I got the job a few years earlier on the recommendation of one of her clients, a resort comic who owed me a few favors.

My first impression of Hilary Quayle was mixed. Physically, I found her extremely appealing: sky-blue eyes, long graceful neck, pale blond silky hair that she used to tie severely in back, but now lets fall loosely in soft parentheses about her delicately complexioned face. Though petite, she is well curved, dressing tastefully but modestly, yet the most sober business suit whispers contradictions when Hilary wears it.

But somehow Hilary's beauty irritates her. She reminds me a little of St. Bridget, distracted from what she thought her true self by the accident of comeliness. Like Bridget, Hilary found a way of offsetting the attribute: sarcasm of so virulent a strain that at first she seems as warm and charming as a copperhead. It took me quite a while (though it was worth the wait) to glimpse the caring, vulnerable woman behind the facade, and to recognize Hilary as one of those blithely tormented people who never really know their own beauty and try to hide their uncertainty behind a rampart of bravado and irony.

Hilary is a frustrated detective. It stems from a tangled need to both emulate and surpass her father, himself a prominent Manhattan private investigator. He left Hilary and her mother when she was a girl, and ever since she's tried to win Daddy's approval—or at least, his notice. Once she offered to work for him for nothing so she could learn his business, but—equating her offer with the price —he refused with an offhand contempt that has smoldered in her ever since.

The stumbling block to her ambition is New York's stipulation that an applicant must work three years at existing detective agencies before being eligible for a license. She's tried to hold down such jobs, but never managed to last long. She blames her father, thinks he pulled strings to get her fired, but I find that doubtful. I don't think he'd go to that much trouble on her account. More likely, her mouth just rammed broadside some very unliberated male employers.

The early days as Hilary's assistant were strained. She fired me more than once, and I quit a few times, but little by little, a romantic bond began to grow between us, maybe not as strong as the one the dwarfs fashioned to bind the wolf, but tight enough to chafe us both. We were Mirabell and Millamant, afraid to climb down from our self-images and admit we liked each other. A case of love at first spite.

I got the bright idea to renew my old detective's license, a relic of upstate unemployment from one of my many abortive pasts. I thought it would be the perfect way to help Hilary achieve her dream. "All you have to do," I told her, "is chuck PR and open up an investigative bureau with me as figurehead, you as brains. Once you earn your license as my 'employee,' you can assume your rightful place as agency head. What do you think?"

"I think," she replied acidulously, "that you want to change a symbiotic relationship to a parasitic one with myself as host body."

That left her open to two cracks, one sexist, one psychological. I was so stung by her attitude that I used them both, and as usual, she fired me. It didn't take, though. A week later, an old friend of hers called and on a rare impulse, Hilary asked me along for a few drinks at Mr. William Shakespeare's in the Village. It was the beginning of the sequence of events elsewhere chronicled as *Bullets for Macbeth*, and it ended with me and Hilary as lovers. Our honeymoon lasted until last June. I made the mistake of inviting Hilary to the annual banquet of Sons of the Desert, the international Laurel and Hardy society. I'm a member of the New York founding "tent," which until recently was strictly stag. Hilary found out, called me a sexist and refused to speak to me for days on end. The result was *The Laurel and Hardy Murders* and a change of membership policy at Sons of the Desert.

But by the time Hilary and I reconciled, my old job was filled. Not that I was out of work; while the deep freeze was on, I accepted an offer from Frank Butler, "The Old Man," the worst excuse for a detective in the East. I was sure it was a temporary situation, but then I suppose every employee thinks himself absolutely irreplaceable, so when Hilary gave my job to Harry Whelan, I was stunned. Also jealous. Harry is a part-time actor and full-time opportunist. He dated Hilary and went with her on a business trip to Washington that I've never felt easy about. I was sure he hadn't gotten her out of his system. It's difficult.

One week before the night I sat gawking at my goldfish I was on the phone with Hilary having an old argument. She assured me for the hundredth time that I'd have my old job back as soon as Harry left. She'd been telling it to me for a long time. I figured it was time for her to make a token move to prove there was still something between us. Firing Harry would be a nice gesture.

"Has it occurred to you," I asked her on the phone, "that dear Harry may not be pursuing his acting career quite so zealously these days?"

"Gene, you know it's not unusual for an actor to be unemployed for long stretches of time."

"Correction, milady—Harry *is* employed. He's just not acting."

"Are you implying," she asked in her Number Two Icicle Voice, "that my relationship with him is anything other than professional?"

"No. Should I?"

A brief pause. Then in too precise diction she told me she refused to discuss it further. "If *you* want to wallow in neurotic projection, Gene, that's—"

I whistled appreciatively. "Neurotic projection? An area of considerable expertise on your part, milady."

I had the phone away from my ear before she slammed it down.

So I was still stuck in Philly earning peanuts from the laughable Benjamin F. Butler a/k/a The Old Man.

But exactly one day after the long-distance spat with Hilary, my resort comic pal—the one who first recommended me to Hilary—rang me up with the news that none other than Harry Whelan just signed a one-year contract with Colson-Ames Productions to play an ongoing part on (of all shows) the WBS-TV daytime drama—soap opera, if you insist—"Riverday."

I'd often ribbed The Old Man for his addiction to "Days of Our Lives," etc., but while he was out of town, he told me to videotape his favorite programs. That's when I came out of the closet and got hooked on "Riverday." It and "Ryan's Hope" proved my downfall, partly because both are extremely well written, partly because I became enamored of an actress on "Riverday." Her name is Lara Wells, and she bears an uncanny resemblance to Hilary Quayle. Of which, more anon.

Well, I rejoiced, *it finally happened. Harry Whelan is a working actor once more!* He'd promised Hilary he'd move out once he found employment in his own field, so my old job finally was vacant and ready for me.

Only why hadn't she called to ask me back? I gave her the benefit of the doubt and assumed she hadn't known about Harry's contract when she hung up on me. I decided to sit tight and wait for her to phone with the news.

I waited all week.

On Friday afternoon, I swallowed my pride and called her, but got her answering machine. That tended to confirm the report. Hilary dislikes using the recorder unless there's no way she can leave the office manned. *So Harry must be gone*, I thought.

The beep sounded. I stammered a message of apology for what I'd recently said to her on the phone. It took too long, but before the allotted half-minute elapsed, I managed to squeeze in a question: did she have anything to tell me?

I could've saved myself the trouble. It fetched no response. She didn't call at all that day, Friday. Or the next day, either, the Saturday of the goldfish and the news bulletin.

I waited till evening, then my patience ditto temper ran out. Around 10:30 P.M. I left another message on Hilary's answering machine. I had no trouble whatsoever fitting it into the thirty-second time limit.

Because I had Harry on my mind, "Riverday" was already there, too. After I left my rude message, I settled down with the Philadelphia *Inquirer*, the edition for that Saturday, and while leafing through it, saw a two-page spread with a headline at least forty-two points high.

MEET YOUR FAVORITE SOAP OPERA STARS!

Want to meet your favorite Soap Stars IN PERSON? Find out what they're REALLY, REALLY LIKE? Get behind-the-camera lowdown on THEIR private lives? Here's your chance . . .

There was a lot more copy, but the gist was that six men and a like number of women—performers representing all twelve current "soaps"—would be in the flesh Sunday from one o'clock on to greet the public and answer questions at the brand-new Delaware County Shopping Mall, twenty miles southeast of downtown Philly.

The representative for "Riverday" was Lara Wells, the Hilary Quayle lookalike I had a crush on.

The newspaper ad reminded me I hadn't yet viewed Friday's "Riverday" episode. Idly wondering whether Harry was on it, I fished it out of the holder and turned on the set, but before I had a chance to flick over to playback mode, my three goldfish caught my eye. It was about ten minutes before 11 P.M.

Charlie was my first fish. A next-door neighbor bequeathed him (her?) to me. At that time he lived in a variety store fishbowl, the kind you can hold in one hand. Deciding Charlie would be lonely in there, I bought her (him?) a companion, but the newcomer lasted less than a week. It occurred to me I didn't know all that much about goldfish care, so—dumping the dead fish and changing the water—I bought a paperback on *How to Help Your Goldfish Thrive*. I found out what I was doing wrong. Everything.

Ninety dollars later, Charlie was comfortably ensconced in a ten-gallon aquarium filled with aged tap water, a filter floss/charcoal corner filter, fifteen pounds of prewashed gravel, a hose leading to the air pump that rests above on the tank's screen cover (which also holds the 25-watt strip light), two fantails named Marty and Jackie, and a batch of anchored anarchis.

According to the book, anarchis is a hardy plant capable of withstanding the nibbling of the average goldfish. It didn't have a chance with my roughnecks, though. I stared at them for at least ten minutes while they tore off every single leaf from every available stalk. I wondered whether they were engaged in some kind of Pet Power protest. Maybe they wanted a bigger aquarium? Different food?

The Channel 14 teaser shook me from my reverie. I put down the VTR cartridge and waited for the commercials to end. Soon the newscaster returned and the remote film played. I saw a vaguely familiar midtown Manhattan block. An ambulance was at the curb. There were police holding back the curious.

"This afternoon at a quarter past two, a man fell from the roof of the block-long WBS-TV studios on West Fifty-third Street near Twelfth Avenue. Medical examiners say he died instantly.

"Police refuse to comment on whether the death was accidental, suicide or the result of deliberate violence. However, Chief Inspector Lou Betterman admitted the incident looks extremely suspicious."

The familiar boiled-fish glower of Fat Lou Betterman, Hilary's family friend on the force, appeared on the screen. Brushing his stubby thumb back and forth over the straggly ends of his salt/pepper mustache, Betterman spoke into the handheld microphone the remotecaster aimed at him.

BETTERMAN (grousing)
Look, I'm not bugged because the victim happened to be bare-[BLEEP], it's a hot day, maybe he was sunbathing. But I want to know where the [BLEEP] his clothes are, we didn't find 'em on the roof.

The camera panned to the remote reporter, who said further investigation disclosed nobody had seen a man without clothes wandering the WBS halls.

They cut to another on-the-spot interview, this time with an elderly security guard wearing glasses so thick his eyes looked three times as big as they actually must have been.

SECURITY GUARD

. . . a hell of a lot, man, not on a Saturday, 'cause they don't tape "Riverday" on th' weekend, there's just only th' news crew, and they's all accounted for. That poor bastard must've just snuck in—

Which amounted to a general announcement that WBS security was lax and the public might as well come right over and nose around. I felt sorry for the old man. He probably just bought himself a pink slip.

The anchorman returned and said the body, too badly smashed to identify, was at the ME's on First Avenue, where the usual fingerprinting, tissue samples and forensic dentistry work was under way.

I had my fill of atrocity news. Switching to VTR mode, I inserted the tape cartridge and settled back to watch "Riverday."

It was a good episode. Lara Wells had several dramatic scenes that gave her a chance to show what fine acting she was capable of. I marveled once more at her uncanny resemblance to Hilary. They even shared a few mannerisms.

No evidence on the program of Harry Whelan. It was a good episode.

I dozed off before it was over. In my sleep, I rescued Lara from man-eating telephones and a horde of naked goldfish.

hmmmmmmmmmmmmmmmmmmmmmmmmmmmmmmm

It's bad enough to fall asleep feeling sorry for yourself, but it's a hell of a lot worse waking up in the same state with a stiff neck from sleeping at an impossible angle on a hushed Sunday morning. In Philadelphia.

The VTR, after running to the end of the reel, shut itself off, and now the glowing screen was blank. The speaker emitted a middle-register monotonous hum.

hmmmmmmmmmmmmmmmmmmmmmmmmmmmmmmm

I stood up, cramped and cranky, aching in every joint, rested but not at rest. I could hardly straighten my neck or back. My clothes were rumpled, and I felt gamy. I didn't like myself, the world, or even my goldfish—why should I, they never bought *me* dinner.

I switched off the TV, put away the tape cartridge, went into the bathroom, brushed my teeth, then stripped and let the needlepoint shower try to wash away my predawn blues.

But half an hour later—cleaner, wide awake—I sat once more in my living room, still thoroughly depressed. Once upon a time, Sundays were reserved for reading the funnies on the floor with Dad, eating the banquet maternally labored at all day in the presence of cousins and grandparents, but now they were nothing more than bleak weekly reminders that I was thirtyish, still single, tormented by better yesterdays. My friends are settled, moved or dead, my family is gone, it's gauche to buy newspapers with rotogravure if you can even find them, American restaurants don't have tables for one . . . and even I was bored by the valid yet commonplace litany of my own self-pity.

The late August sun filtered through the interstices of the oriental screening, unaccompanied by the slightest noise of traffic. Pine Street might have been an empty Kansas plain.

After feeding the fish, throwing out the garbage, watching strangers walk past my window, I wondered what device I could discover to take the cutting edge off living through another Sunday.

Stooping, I picked up Saturday's newspaper where I'd left it, still spread out wide upon the living room rug, and there was the big banner headline staring up at me.

MEET YOUR FAVORITE SOAP OPERA STARS!

At first I told myself, Gene, you're not going to drive twenty miles and rubberneck with the unwashed multitudes just to catch a glimpse of your dream-mistress' eyebrow. Then I modified my machismo. I had nothing better to do, and I'd been meaning to check out the new Delaware County mall, anyway. Sure, I felt a little sheepish about the extent to which soap opera addiction had taken hold of my imagination, and yes, I fully expected to find myself in the middle of an army of closet loonies unable to separate fantasy from reality, but damn it, I argued with myself, there are supposed to be fifty-five million Americans watching daytime dramas every week, why should they be any less correct than the proverbial outnumbered Frenchmen?

Before I left, I considered taking along my binoculars, so I could at least be reasonably sure of getting a good look at Lara Wells—just to see if she *really* resembled Hilary all that much. But I decided finally to leave them behind, on the unlikely chance that I might actually meet her. I wouldn't want to give her the impression I'm just another celebrity chaser.

I pulled off Township Line and headed south towards Garrett. Traffic was unusually heavy for a suburban Sunday. I had the ominous impression that most of it was headed exactly where I wanted to go.

I was right. A block away from the main parking lot entrance, the line of autos came to a bumper-to-bumper standstill. It took a good ten minutes to inch close enough to see the actual turnoff. The holdup was chiefly caused by a few inept lot attendants trying to direct the arriving vehicles to the rapidly disappearing spaces within.

I managed to make it inside, though not many behind me did. I found a space in the last, furthest row from the long, low line of the exterior mall. Switching off the ignition, I locked up, got out and set off for the main entrance.

It was a warm afternoon, with a sky the color of the water of Provincetown. The clouds were shy and scant, and the sun gloried in puckering up my eyes against its glare.

As I drew closer to the quarter-mile-long main el of the complex, I realized that, despite the crowd, I was in a much better mood, partly because I was doing something instead of sitting at home staring at the calcimine, partly because the clement weather brightened me. But mainly because I enjoy visiting shopping centers, department stores, supermarkets—they evoke in me that sense of Carnival which is an apt metaphor for America itself, glamorous and tawdry and wonderful. Even roadside Howard Johnsons charm me with their vulgar array of coin machines that I can never pass without dropping in a quarter just to witness the mechanical mysteries of some worthless trinket's chuted delivery.

In the parking lot, adults and children of all ages streamed towards the mall's main entrance, bottlenecking before its thick Lucite portals like dreamers asked to choose between the Gates of Ivory or Horn. Their eager shining faces were mostly Caucasian, but with a generous sprinkling of other ethnic groups. Some talked and laughed, but mostly it was a curiously quiet crowd, tense with a charged anticipation that was palpable in the air of early afternoon.

When still some distance from the entry, I observed a riptide of countermovement about twenty feet to my right. An eddy of autograph-seekers waving papers, books, pens and pencils converged on a young blonde vainly attempting to push through the knot of people.

My breath caught. I immediately recognized Lara Wells' silky hair, tied severely back, her trim figure, her lustrous blue eyes. But how in hell could Security permit her to walk unescorted across a thronged parking lot? It was madness. The fans would strip and smother her in the name of adulation.

I white-knighted to her side, elbowing, sidling, shoving and trampling, skipping sidesaddle. Her distressed voice wailed above the crowd's gabble. Middle-aged women shook crimson-leather autograph books in her face; hands dipped into Lara's purse and the dossier she carried beneath one arm, emerging with photographs, lipstick, rouge, even wadded tissues. A teenager with acne used the press of the mob as an excuse to familiarize himself with her contours. She huddled in a defenseless ball, her eyes wide with panic.

Muscling in next to her, managing to accidentally on

purpose knock aside the kid and a few of the more rabid
souvenir seekers, I shouted for her to stay close, I was
going to help her break through.

Gratefully, she turned to acknowledge the aid. Then
her eyes widened, and so did mine.

"Gene!" Hilary exclaimed, throwing her arms around
my neck.

Every action has an equal and opposite reaction, and
Hilary was running true to form. Yes, she thanked me for
the cosmetics I purchased to replace what her "fans"
filched. But it bothered her that I knew all her brands
and shades.

We sat across the table from one another exchanging
cool trivialities while elsewhere in the mall's third-floor
press room half a dozen daytime celebrities told polite
fictions to journalists. The first "star show" was scheduled
for 1 P.M., the second at four. Because Lara Wells was in
the early lineup, she was downstairs getting ready and I
had not yet set eyes on her.

The large, chilly room was filled with white linen-
covered round tables that bore small bowls of potato
chips, popcorn, pretzels and peanuts. A much-frequented
bar was stocked with all the basics. Against one wall was
a long banquet table laden with great trays of cold cuts,
naked shrimp ringing reservoirs of cocktail sauce, cherry
tomatoes and celery stalks and stuffed olives, wilted let-
tuce beds cradling diced fruit assortments, here and there
a crabapple included for shape and color. But one of
them graced the platter I brought to Hilary.

As I glanced across the table at her, I marveled at how
much lovelier she was in person than memory painted
her, even though my recollection kept her likeness in
cameo. Her light golden hair shone with dazzling high-

lights and her blue eyes seemed to hint at things her lips refused to utter.

Earlier, Lara herself loaned Hilary a pair of slacks and appropriate blouse to replace the dress that the mob rumpled and ripped. Meanwhile, I shopped in a variety store downstairs and found the irritating cosmetics.

Hilary was determined to minimize my rescue. "I could have handled those animals," she said, "but they all seemed to think I was Lara, and that meant I had to keep my temper. Otherwise, whatever I did would have been blamed on my cousin, and ugly rumors would get into the fanzines."

"Uh-huh," I agreed drily, nibbling at a Saltine. If that's how she chose to play it, okay, there was no need for me to edit her own personal filmtrack of events the way she wanted to remember them. And if she didn't wish to bring up Harry, that was all right, too. For the time being.

"So Lara Wells is actually your cousin Lainie."

"Mm-hmm. On my mother's side. We grew up together, but she was Laraine Adler in those days. We've been out of touch nearly ten years."

Laraine Adler. Cousin Lainie. I'd often heard the name. Hilary doesn't talk much about her girlhood, unless to complain about her father. But on those infrequent occasions that find Hilary in a rare nostalgic mood, she usually mentions her cousin Lainie—Laraine—with a mixture of affection and envy. Lara née Laraine was a breezy, outgoing, assertive young woman; everything Hilary wasn't and wished she could be. Hilary constantly argued with her mother, but Lainie got away with lots of things without ever being caught or scolded. Oddly, Hilary never considered it unfair; she loved her cousin and secretly vowed to be more like her when she grew older.

I had no idea if she'd succeeded, but I always thought it'd be interesting to meet Lainie and compare her with Hilary. Nothing ever was said about Lainie being an actress, so it didn't dawn on me that Lara's uncanny resemblance to Hilary was anything but coincidence.

Sipping at her Kirin beer, Hilary told me she got a phone call from Lara several weeks after I took a job at Butler's Djinn Investigations in Philadelphia. "The two of us got together and talked over ancient history. I agreed to handle Lara's PR, but that wasn't till after I helped get her work on 'Riverday.'"

"How'd you manage that?" I asked, amazed. Soap casting is very much of a closed-shop affair.

"Do you remember Abel Harrison?"

"Trim-Tram Toys? Sure."

"He left Trim-Tram and formed his own ad agency. Recently he diversified into talent."

Harrison was a wispy nebbish who kept his tenure at the toy firm because he was the president's brother-in-law. Otherwise, he was a family thorn, a genius at botching every assignment. But then Hilary got mixed up in a small problem of industrial thievery at the company, and by the time she unraveled things, Harrison inherited the ad department. He surprised everyone, himself included, by showing remarkable eptness for the field.

"Harrison Talent," Hilary continued, "is the new name of Maggert-Axel, which Abel bought out. Now he supplies extras for a lot of East Coast films and does all the casting for 'Riverday.' I called in an old debt and got Lara her part."

I suppressed an urge to ask whether she also helped Harry onto the show.

The press room door opened. A dapper man entered. Trim, dark, with close-cropped curly brown hair and a narrow nose supporting black spectacles, he was, according to Hilary, Barry Clover, publicity coordinator for, and partner in CloverLeaf Shows, the major producer of soap festivals throughout the country—specializing in anything from ticketed bruncheons accommodating perhaps a hundred hard-core fans to free monster rallies like the one I was attending. The latter events, I was told later, draw anywhere from six thousand to ten thousand people in a single day.

Clover stepped to the floor mike, gently tapped it to make sure it was "live," then said, "The one o'clock show begins in ten minutes. I'll lead anyone who wants to see it to the reserved press section in front. Those of you in the middle of interviews don't have to rush if you don't want to. The press room's open all day, the food'll keep coming, and the bar won't run dry."

An audible sigh from the working press.

Hilary finished her beer and stood. "I have to watch the show. Want to see how Lara does?"

I nodded, though my feelings were mixed. I would have liked to be alone with Hilary. But I wanted to meet my dream girl, too, preferably without Hilary hanging over me. That, of course, was now impossible. As Lara's PR agent, Hilary would be right at my elbow. It also occurred to me that Hilary wouldn't much like it if she knew my reason for coming to the mall. She'd assumed my fortuitous arrival to be nothing more than a geographical coincidence. She has the typical New Yorker's Lilliputian concept of the size of Philadelphia.

Clover led us to the parking lot and beyond to the far end of the mall, where we came upon some enormous bleachers set up in front of a bunting-draped platform. The seats were jampacked. Clover turned us over to the ushers, who took us to a reserved *VIP* section down front. As I sat, I felt the hostile glares of the *UIPs* directly behind me.

The platform was empty except for a long table bearing name cards that corresponded to the six as-yet-unseen celebrities. The second sign from center stage read LARA WELLS.

A fortyish woman with just enough weight on her hips to render her Kewpie-doll squeezable climbed onto the platform, smiled nervously at the audience and crossed to the down-right microphone, audibly clearing her throat. She wore a simple floral-print frock, had frosted blond hair and deep dimples and clutched a seed-pearl purse beneath her left arm. She looked like an elementary school librarian browbeaten into addressing a mothers' workshop on her day off.

Speaking with a vaguely midwestern twang, she introduced herself as Honey Leaf, hostess of the festival.

"Some actress herself, *n'est-ce pas?*" Hilary whispered.

I nodded. I'd met Mrs. Clover briefly in the press room: a highstrung articulate woman, smartly dressed and without a trace of accent. The person onstage looked dowdy and thoroughly ingenuous, a comfortable interlocutor that the women in the audience could identify with, and perhaps feel slightly superior to.

Honey (actually Helen) welcomed everyone and explained that the tickets they received upon entry were their chances "for a real special bunch o' door prizes!" Then she began her first introduction. "Ladies, y'all seen his rugged good looks for a couple seasons on 'The Edge of Night' and lots o' commercials, but today he's better known as Dr. Ellis Peters on 'Brighter Morrow'—Alan Emory!"

Thunderous applause. Cheers, whistles. Women screamed. Before the ushers could stop her, a young girl in jeans ran forward and scattered rose petals in the air. A trim, tall man with wavy light brown hair stepped onstage and acknowledged the ovation with an ease that showed he fully expected and deserved such adulation. He said hello in a voice that none of his fans loved half so much as himself. More ecstatic squeals.

As he sat, Hilary murmured a line of Dickens, "'As for bowing down in body and spirit, nothing was left for Heaven.'"

I didn't comment. I was listening to the second introduction.

"—exciting new daytime star, an adorable little lady who brings special glamour to Women's Lib with her portrayal of Roberta Jennett on 'Riverday'—Ms. Lara Wells!"

Another round of applause, less overwhelming than the first, chiefly due to the absence of distaff histrionics, though Lara garnered her share of wolf whistles. *La belle dame* of my dreams appeared. Her resemblance to Hilary really was remarkable: the same light silken hair, the same sky-blue eyes, similarly petite but amply curved figure. Lara wore a sedate green tweed suit, a scratchy material I've never seen the use of, but on her it looked good, it clung.

Four other soap stars were subsequently introduced, but I didn't pay much attention to them, I was too busy glancing back and forth between Lara and Hilary.

"Yes, I know," Hilary said with sardonic amusement, "but turn around, you're not at a tennis match."

So I focused on Lara, which was no hardship. It was easy to get lost in the depths of her wide, gentle eyes. There was a quality about her, a vulnerability that Hilary fought to cover up in herself. As Honey Leaf asked warmup questions of the celebrities, Lara fielded hers ably, but with a diffidence that was a pleasing contrast to the forthright manner of the part she played on "Riverday." Hilary perfected: the charm without the emasculatory instinct.

Honey turned the probing over to the audience. Ushers took up posts in the bleachers, each equipped with hand-held mikes which they directed at spectators waving hands in the air.

Some of the things they asked were rather personal, but the stars remained affable, probably afraid of the press they'd get if they allowed themselves to be flapped by the prying. But most of the questions were of the harmless "slambook" variety: "What's your favorite color/song/TV show/movie/food/sport/etc.?"

A handful of queries were more sophisticated. One woman wanted to find out how far ahead the actors know what's going to happen on their respective programs.

Alan Emory, next to Lara, said, "About three weeks. That's the usual taping schedule, right?" The rest of the panel agreed. "The head writer, the producer, and maybe the sponsor, if there's one powerful enough, work up a projected storyline, or 'Bible' for the next six months or a year. It's top secret, the actors don't get to see it."

"It's better that we don't," Lara put in.

"Right," he nodded. "Our job is to make it look as if things are taking place for the first time. With the crazy work schedules we have, that's almost how it works out, too. Anyway, what happens is the head writer is in charge of the 'Bible' storyline, which he breaks down, week after week, into daily synopses which episode writers turn into the actual shooting scripts. The producer's staff stats these and passes them out to the cast."

"If you play a major role," Lara added, "you have to learn so many lines nearly every night that you don't find time to read anything but the scenes you're in. That's why we often don't know what's happening to other characters in the story. It's a lot like life."

The Q-A session lasted most of the hour. At ten of two, the drawing was held for merchandise donated by various mall shops, but the prizes proved of secondary importance—for as the guest stars fished the lucky numbers from a big bowl, the winners bustled onstage and collected, along with their loot, a romantic embrace from whichever celebrity he or she preferred. It struck me as odd that a kiss could be so important to one person and nothing more than a public relations gesture to the other partner.

The jerk who hugged Lara too close looked a little like Harry Whelan.

Back upstairs in the press room, the questions flung at the performers were more incisive. I stood behind Lara and listened with Hilary as the actress wound up an interview with a reporter from *Grit*.

"There's an enormous difference," she told him, "between our viewers' fantasies of the world we move in, and the actuality. There's not much day-to-day glamour in acting on a soap."

The reporter skeptically asked her to expand on her remark.

Lara brushed a strand of blond hair from her forehead. "I have to be in the studio by seven A.M. to start on my makeup. By eight or eight-thirty, we're in the greenroom rehearsing, after which we go downstairs for camera blocking. I get my hair done for the dress rehearsal, and then we tape. Late lunch, I stop in the office for the next day's script, which averages forty or fifty pages of lines to learn on a heavy day. I go home and study, eat dinner and go to bed no later than nine-thirty because I've got to get up at five A.M. to be ready for the studio limo. Sound glamorous?"

The reporter allowed it seemed pretty grim. He wondered why anyone would want such a life.

Lara shrugged. "Security. If I worked every week of the year on Broadway at Equity scale, I'd barely be able to survive. Soaps pay well, and they're steady work."

"Except when they decide to kill off a character, right?"

She wrinkled her nose. "That's a subject I'd rather not think about."

"If you had to do something other than 'Riverday,' what would it be?"

A smirk. "Skydiving. The risks are similar."

Before the next interview, Hilary introduced me to her cousin. Lara rose, clasped both my hands and stared at me, amazed, as if I'd just materialized from insubstantial air.

"Gene? *The* Gene? You actually exist?"

"Lainie," murmured Hilary, "behave . . ."

Her cousin ignored her. "Gene, it's really *you?*"

"Last time I looked." I didn't know what she was getting at, but it was the kind of arch teasing I generally dislike. I didn't mind it as much, though, coming from Lara.

"You see," she said, "I thought you were a figment of Hilary's imagination."

"Sometimes I am," I admitted, nodding at Hilary, who granted me a frosty twitch of the lips. It was strange standing between them, like talking to both images in a looking-glass. They could have been mirror twins.

"Hilary constantly chatters about you, Gene—"

Lara ignored the nudge in her ribs.

"—but after all these months, I couldn't decide whether she made you up, or just wanted to keep us apart. I steal all her boyfriends, you know."

A harder nudge. Paying no attention, Lara gave me a

peck on the cheek. "Welcome to the family, Gene." That did it. Hilary pivoted on her heel and walked away. Lara smiled at her retreating back. "I never could resist."

"She can't handle teasing on personal subjects like men."

"Never could." Lara regarded me appraisingly. "Underneath the thin ice, though, Hilary's honest and decent and has a lot of love." A shrug. "She's damned special. I hope you know what you've got."

I cocked an eyebrow. "I'm not aware I have anything. Especially lately. And she'll be the first to say she's not a possession."

"That, love, is only the lady's press handout."

Listening to Lara, I felt disoriented. For the moment, she was one hundred and eighty degrees removed from the woman I couldn't stop watching on "Riverday." She was Hilary's cousin, that's all. Though I *was* fascinated by her lips; they formed her words so carefully, shaping every vowel with machined precision, crisply shearing off the consonants. She also had impeccable placement. There was a velvet texture to her voice, a caress of sound that came from her diaphragm, curving to the back of her throat before lips and tongue and teeth gentled it into words. Her technique was smooth enough to seem artless, the effortlessness of endless years of practice.

"I think," she was saying, "that you still have a few things to learn about Hilary."

"And vice versa."

"Very likely." She lowered her voice to a conspiratorial whisper. "And I imagine Hilary told you all sorts of salacious stories about me?"

"Your name *has* come up. But I never connected you with Cousin Lainie."

"Hm?"

"With Lara Wells."

She eyed me curiously. "You've seen me act?"

"Every afternoon, five days a week."

A peal of merry laughter, followed by an impulsive squeeze of my arm. "Gene, I'm sorry! It's just that you don't strike me as a typical soap opera addict."

"I'm not, I'm a Lara Wells addict."

"Sweet blarney, love." She puckered her lips into a kiss. "But you only say that because I look like Hilary."

"Well, not so much up close." It was true. Subtle telltales distinguished her. Lara's cheeks were flatter, hinting at an elongation that the years would probably accentuate. Her eyes were more heavily lidded than Hilary's; they lent her an aura of mystery, of imperfectly suppressed sensuality. Unlike her cousin's refractive gaze, Lara looked at me frankly, sizing me up and ultimately accepting me without any hint she might prefer me some other way. An important difference.

The banter continued. "Gene, I adore your hyperbole, but it's actually baloney. You don't watch me every day, I'm only on a few times a week."

"Granted. Which is why I never miss an episode. Just in case."

"God!" She laughed. "Keep that up and I'll drag you off to my cave! However, according to all the national polls," Lara stated in the flat metal timbre and clockwork rhythms of a computerized message, "the average soap viewer only tunes in two or three times a week." She resumed her normal voice. "I admit you're way above average, love, that's what Hilary claims, but if you really watch me every afternoon, when do you find time to work?"

"All right, I confess! I watch at night on a VTR."

She rolled her eyes in pretended panic. "Omigod, you're not a fan, you're a fanatic! Call out Security!"

Abandoning the badinage, I asked whether the statistic she'd cited was really true.

"Sure is. Why do you think they give us all those boring recaps? 'Roberta, did you know Matt's having an affair with blahblahblah?' *That* sort of thing."

"Which I've noticed there's less of on 'Riverday' than some other shows."

"Uh-huh. That's one of the reasons Ed won so many Emmies. And probably a contributing factor to our fight for audience share. It keeps slipping." She brooded on it briefly, then waved it away as Hilary reappeared with Lara's next scheduled interviewer.

The latter individual was an ax-faced andiron named Jess Brass, a bony, humorless woman who serves as chief critic and gossip columnist for the New York *Daily Lineup*, a raggy tabloid with an unwholesomely large circulation. Her column, "Daylong Lineup," consists of plot synopses and behind-the-scenes scandal about the soaps. Brass has a talent for stinging innuendo that places her high among the apostles of the John Simon method of criticism, which holds that viciousness is an apt substitute for percipience. She is a small, insecure woman whose narrow spirit envies and resents most of the actresses her position forces her to notice in print . . . which she does by mining the dungheap of her own neuroses. Her column, of course, is enormously popular. Compost always draws flies.

The angular woman put a folded newspaper on a tabletop and sat down to interview Lara with as much enthusiasm as an intern preparing to dissect decomposing tissue. As Lara took the opposite seat, Hilary tugged my sleeve and drew me away.

"Brass won't begin till we leave," she said. Nodding, I followed her to the bar and ordered a Bushmill's. I knew

Hilary still was bristly from Lara's chaffing, so I tried to establish a truce by clinking my glass against hers, but she just glared at me.

"Well, what are you smirking about, brightness?"

I took a sip to control my temper. "Look, Hilary, I'm attempting to maintain a diplomatic silence."

"Really? Then you'd better stop thinking so loud."

"Thoughtcrime won't be a statutory offense till 1984."

If she had a comeback, for once I was spared hearing it. Suddenly ignoring me, Hilary looked across the room. Her brows drew down.

Turning to see what was the matter, I observed Lara, still at the table, sitting with rigid back and wide-staring eyes. There was no color in her cheeks.

Hilary hurried over. "Lara, what's wrong?" No answer.

The folded newspaper Jess Brass brought with her was open beneath the actress' nose. Hilary snatched it from the columnist's grasp.

I peered over Hilary's shoulder and saw a single-column, three-deck page-three headline stripped over a photograph of a good-looking man with long dark hair, pencil-line mustache and glasses.

I read the headline and story.

POLICE IDENTIFY
TV WRITER AS
NUDE FALL VICTIM

Medical examiners told police today that the naked man who fell to his death yesterday afternoon from the roof of the Manhattan studios of WBS-TV on West 53rd Street is Edward Niven, 43, award-winning head writer of "Riverday," a "soap opera" taped daily in the block-long broadcasting complex.

NYPD Chief Inspector Louis Betterman said that though Niven's office is in the same building there is no explanation why he should have been on the roof on a weekend, when "Riverday" is not in production.

"He didn't sign in at the security desk," the police officer stated. "Nobody knows when he arrived, or why he avoided entering the front way."

No explanation has been tendered for Niven's nakedness. No clothing was found on the roof.

The report ended with a few facts about Niven's long career as a daytime drama writer, and how he'd consistently won the Emmy for "Riverday," a show he held a part interest in.

Typical generalist reportage, I mused sourly. The questions the reporter didn't ask Lou Betterman could've filled as many column inches as the article already occupied.

"Gene," Hilary said, "take Lara away. She and Ed were good friends."

As I guided the stricken actress to the door, Hilary eased Jess Brass to a neutral corner without actually breaking her fingers.

"That bitch!" Lara spoke low, but with great vehemence. I silently agreed with her assessment of Jess Brass.

I stayed with Lara till Hilary joined us and took over. I retired to another part of the room while the cousins whispered to one another. Hilary did her best to calm Lara. The love they had for one another shone through; they shared a sisterly closeness.

Soon, Lara felt she could handle the rest of her interviews, Brass excluded. The actress' earlier sparkle was gone, but she went through the necessary motions and was done by half-past three. Hilary suggested late lunch, but Lara wasn't hungry.

"I'd better call New York. The producer might be trying to reach me."

"But it's Sunday," I reminded her.

"Makes no difference. The Ames office may have left a message on my service, what with—what with Ed's death." She drew a ragged breath. "And I'd better call Florence, too."

"Why?" Hilary asked, an element of surprise in her voice.

"Because she's probably falling apart."

I asked whether she was talking about Florence McKinley, lead actress on "Riverday."

"Yes," Lara nodded. "She and Ed were lovers."

"All right," I suggested, "why not stop at my place, it's more or less on your way back to New York, anyway. I'll fix us drinks, supper if you like, and you can use my phone undisturbed."

Lara said she'd appreciate it. She got into Hilary's car and they followed me as I threadneedled my private route around City Line, avoiding most of the major traffic traps. We reached Pine Street by ten after four.

Whatever prompted me to put a picture of Lara on my wall, I'll never know. A few months earlier, I saw an attractive color photo of her on the cover of *Soap Opera Digest,* the Tiffany periodical of the soap genre. On impulse, I bought the issue and read about her. Nothing in the article connected her with Hilary, of course. Eventually I tossed out the magazine, but the cover—carefully trimmed to eliminate the male costar posed with Lara—now was taped above my desk.

Lara saw it as soon as I opened the door. Her eyes widened for a second, glanced into mine, then looked away.

Hilary saw it, too.

Pretending not to notice, I crossed the room, cracked the bedroom door and told Lara the telephone was inside. She thanked me, pressed my hand in passing, and walked into the other room, closing the door behind her.

"What would you like to drink?" I asked Hilary.

"The usual," she replied too sweetly. "You know me so well."

I tried to overlook her sarcasm, but she had no intention of making it easy. She sat down at my desk, put her chin in her hands, rested her elbows on the desk top and gazed adoringly at Lara's picture.

"All right, all right, I'll take it down."

"Did I ask you to? It's your apartment, you're certainly permitted to decorate it the way you like."

"Hilary, knock it off."

She raised an eyebrow. "Did I say something wrong? I beg your pardon! From now on, I'll maintain a diplomatic silence."

"I said I'd take it down."

"But I regard it as a compliment. You never asked me for a personal photo. This must be the next best thing."

I yanked it off the wall and tossed it in the wastebasket.

Hilary retreated into aloof nonconversation.

I busied myself with ice, olive, vermouth and Bombay gin. Hilary accepted it without thanks. A good ten minutes elapsed, and neither of us said a word to the other. Once or twice our eyes met, only to slide away to some unimportant object or spot on the wall. I felt like having out the Harry business, but it wouldn't be a good idea to bring it up during the deep freeze. Hilary just might hire someone else out of spite.

Lara finally reemerged from the bedroom.

"Well," Hilary asked, "did you get through?"

The actress nodded, passing a hand across her forehead. There were temporary creases there that the news of Niven's death had brought. She looked a little pale and in need of a friend. I rose and steered her to the sofa.

"What's that?" Lara asked, indicating our half-empty glasses.

"Bombay martinis. Suitable?"

"Thanks, Gene." Her voice was a little hoarse. I fought the urge to put my arm around her shoulder. I wasn't sure if the impulse stemmed from a desire to comfort her or rile Hilary.

I contented myself with mixing another drink and closing Lara's fingers around the glass before sitting down beside her.

She took a long, numbing swallow. Then she leaned back, eyes closed, and spoke. "I have to be on the set an hour earlier tomorrow morning. It's going to be hell till they hire a new head writer."

"But aren't you three weeks ahead on tape, like you said at the mall?" I asked. "Won't that be enough to take up the slack?"

"To replace Ed? No way. If a writer's good enough to be a head writer, he's already working." Draining her glass, she requested a refill. While I mixed another, Lara mused. "We've got about five weeks' grace. Besides fifteen shows already recorded and the five to be taped this week, the office will be copying and distributing next week's scripts to the cast starting late tomorrow or Tuesday. Beyond that, Ed may have given Tommy one or two episode synopses to work on, but production—"

"Tommy?" Hilary interrupted. "The snotty twerp?"

"Uh-huh. Tommy Franklin, *l'enfant terrible*—literally— of the midday mellers. He's our only episode writer now. Ed used to do two thirds of the dailies himself." As she spoke, Lara absently smoothed and resmoothed the green tweed of her skirt over her crossed left leg. It was almost a caress.

"Maybe they'll promote Franklin to head writer?" I said.

"Tommy? Not bloody likely. Ames'll probably have to ask him to rough out a few synopses from what's left of Ed's 'Bible,' but that'll be strictly stopgap. Ames can't stand Tommy. He'd never willingly hire him."

"Sure about that?" Hilary asked.

"Mm-hmm. For one thing, Florence can't stand Tommy, either. If there was ever any question of it, she'd find a way to put a stop to it. She has little tidbits on everyone, and she wouldn't hesitate to use them if her part was threatened."

"Is that how she'd equate Franklin becoming head writer?" I asked.

"Oh, yes. He'd love to do her in, and she knows it."

The conversation lagged. Hilary fished the olive from her glass. Holding it between index finger and thumb, she put it to her lips and sucked out the pimiento, a habit of hers that drives me crazy. The look she gave me then informed me she was well aware of it, and *tant pis*.

She turned to Lara. "You realize your early call tomorrow may have been forced on Ames by the police? You might have to answer a lot of questions."

"Oh, God." A long pause. "Well, I can't tell them very much, can I? I was out of town with you."

"True." Hilary, apparently determined to get on my nerves, repeatedly tapped her forefinger against the rim of her empty glass, each time producing a hollow *ping*. "True. But you can't avoid talking about Ed and Florence."

"I suppose not." Lara's smile was rueful. "Now that Ed's gone, I'm practically the only one left Flo has to talk to."

Hilary did not reply.

Again leaning her head upon the sofa, Lara once more closed her eyes. I observed the rapid swell and fall of her breasts, admired the graceful curve of her long neck, wanted to stroke the silken hair spilling onto her shoulder.

I became acutely aware of Hilary watching me watching Lara.

A silent time passed. I glanced from one cousin to the next, mired in a maze of feelings for them both. I cast about for something else to think about.

Florence McKinley. In her role of Martha Jennett, she held the coveted anchor female part on "Riverday" ever since the program first came on the air. Like Macdonald Carey on "Days of Our Lives," Florence received star billing under the title when the end credits rolled. In the story, Martha was wed to supper club owner Leo Jennett. They had three children: Bella, Matt and Roberta (Lara). Mother Jennett made McKinley an extremely popular character actress with the show's fans because of the warmth and compassion of the character she portrayed. In private, though, she was alleged to be feisty, close with a dollar, and more reclusive than Garbo.

"Did you call her?" Hilary asked.

"Yes. She expects me to come over when we get back tonight."

"You didn't tell her you're coming?"

"Yes."

Hilary clucked her tongue disapprovingly, but refrained from comment.

"Flo's turning Ed's death into her own private melodrama," Lara explained. "She wants me as her audience. Actually, she didn't so much request as command my presence." She finished her drink and put down the glass, olive untouched. "She's sure Ed was murdered."

"*What?*"

I was startled by Hilary's vehemence.

"You heard me. And that's not all. Flo claims she's being set up to take the blame."

I pondered the situation, but all I had was a handful of public facts and lots of unanswered questions. Insufficient data. One of the big things I was curious to know up front was why Lou Betterman, the police inspector, insisted that Niven fell from the roof. How could he be certain the writer didn't jump, or get pushed, from a window?

"Well," said Hilary, flicking her fingertip a final time against her glass before putting it on the coffee table, "if you really can't avoid going out to see her, I'll drive you. Where does she live?"

"Brooklyn Heights." A mirthless smile. "But I have to warn you, you'll stand a better chance of walking into The Oval Office unannounced. Flo probably won't let you come in."

"Then I'll wait in the hall." Hilary stood up. "And to-morrow morning? I ought to sit in on that session, any-way."

"You can try," Lara said doubtfully, "but I don't think they'll let you in there, either."

Hilary was being typical, I thought. Her own high opinion of her detectival skills made her think she could barge in anywhere she wanted.

Lara and I both rose. She smiled apologetically. "Gene, I'm sorry we can't have dinner, but it's a long drive, and I have to see Flo, study my lines and still try not to stay up too late. We soap stars have to go to bed early."

"Making a note of that?" Hilary murmured for my ears only. I ignored her.

Thanking me for the use of the phone, Lara told me to let her know how much she owed when my bill came. Magnanimously, I told her to forget it, duties of a host and all, and instantly felt like kicking myself for passing up a chance to get her phone number.

She gave me a parting peck on the cheek and left. I held the door open for Hilary and, as she walked through, I said, "Tell Harry hello for me."

Back on the other side of the looking-glass, I latched the door, put the glasses in the sink, and fished Lara's photo from the wastebasket.

Dinner was listless, TV was dull. I had a few routine jobs to do on Monday for The Old Man, and frankly looked forward to the petty detail work they'd involve me in. I turned in early, but couldn't fall asleep for a long time. The day and all its questions reran through my mind like videotape.

Shortly past midnight, the telephone roused me from restless slumber.

"Gene?" The voice was sweet, soft, hushed. "Did I wake you?"

In a voice husky from sleep, I asked who it was. "Lara?"

The voice lost its gentle edge. "No, it's her cousin. I got the message you left for me on my machine."

This time, I wasn't fast enough. The sound of Hilary's receiver being slammed down nearly broke my eardrum.

When Lara called me the next evening, I was a little suspicious at first. I thought it was Hilary trying to get even.

Monday was busy. I was out of the office most of the day, and she only crossed my mind once or twice. A minute. Shortly after six, I arrived home and was fumbling with my keys when I heard the ringing of the telephone. I kicked open the door, dropped the groceries on the kitchen counter and hurried into the bedroom to take the call.

I heard a familiar voice on the other end, but didn't take it for granted this time. "Gene," the caller said, "I tried to reach you at your office, but you were out. I've got a big favor to ask."

"Who's calling? Hilary?"

"No, it's Lara." She sounded surprised. "I thought you would recognize my voice."

I didn't know if I'd just wounded her actor's vanity, or if she were leaning a little too literally on the fact that I had her picture on my wall.

"Sorry," I said. "Hilary claims I've got a lousy ear for music. What's the favor?"

"Can you drive up to New York and meet me?"

I caught myself before saying yes and hopping straight into my car. "When? Where?"

"Tonight. At Florence's."

Dream girls don't just call and ask you to drive two hours for a rendezvous. The thing sounded fishy: a sud-

den summons to travel more than a hundred miles to an
unlikely meeting in the home of a woman who turns
strangers from her door. I began to wonder whether I
was really talking to Hilary trying to get even. "This is
awfully short notice," I said. "What's wrong?"

"Florence is really deep-ending Ed's death."

"Okay, but what does that have to do with me?"

"She insists on hiring a detective."

"From another state?"

"Don't you have a New York license?"

"Yes, but that's not the—"

"Hold on, Gene, I'll be right back." I was practically
convinced the call was a trick of Hilary's, but as I waited
impatiently, I heard a second voice talking on the other
end to Lara. Damned if it didn't sound like Florence
McKinley.

"Gene," Lara said in a low voice, "I can't explain now,
she's listening. Look, I know it's expecting an awful lot,
but will you come?"

"Seeing it's you asking, the answer is yes. Give me the
address."

She did, then wondered how long it'd take me to get
there. I estimated a little less than three hours.

Brooklyn Heights, just across the East River from Manhattan, is a sedate, expensive place to live, populated by
many of the financial and municipal workers of Wall
Street and the City Hall district on the other side of the
river. The section extends from the waterfront to its main
business area along Montague Street, which boasts
enough craft shops and exotic restaurants to rival parts
of Greenwich Village.

Most of the streets of "the Heights" are venerable tree-
lined affairs with little in the way of commerce. The
houses include sidewalk-flush apartment buildings as well

as lofty, older residences reachable only by climbing
many steps. Starting out near the decayed elegance of the
once-famous Prince George Hotel (now a chilly husk sur-
mounting a grimy subway depot), walking west, one
passes a profusion of subdued century-old-and-more
homes subdivided into flats facing quaintly named streets
like Orange, Cranberry, and Pineapple. Suddenly, the
river appears hard by a stretch of costly real estate ter-
raced above a long pedestrian promenade. From it,
strollers contemplate the great sweep of Manhattan sky-
line curving south to the harbor where ferries and steam-
ships sail past the Statue of Liberty.

Florence McKinley's apartment was in a steep, narrow
building at the end of a walnut-clustered lane perpendicular to and overhanging the promenade. The last
house on the corner, it was tall and dark and its rear windows sullenly surveyed the public walkway as if disap-
proving of its nearness.

Long before I began watching her on "Riverday," I
knew about Florence McKinley. Her career began during
TV's so-called "golden years," when she performed a
specialty dance on the Ted Mack Amateur Hour. She was
nine years old. Several other bookings followed (I especially remember seeing her on the old Abe Burrows program), and she soon graduated from variety entertainer
to panelist on one of the first quiz shows.

She grew along with the industry, but at eighteen, her
mother pushed her into modeling and then dragged her
to Hollywood, where Florence made a succession of mer-
cifully obscure beach-blanket-and-bikini movies that did
nothing to advance her status as an actress. By the time
she was twenty, she'd disappeared into the wilderness of
touring national companies, community summer stock

and regional dinner theatres. As far as the television industry was concerned, she might never have existed.

Yet nostalgia became fashionable rather soon in the TV medium, perhaps because of the profligacy of airing early shows only once or twice before retiring them to the musty stockpiles of history. Twelve years after her career ended, Florence McKinley returned from the hinterlands and won an Emmy for Best Supporting Actress in "Proud Beauty," a WBS dramatic special. William Morris signed her up, she began doing guest shots on established weekly series, and her face popped up frequently on both late-night and early A.M. talk shows. I saw her on one of the latter just after she'd turned down an offer to be second banana on a new primetime sitcom. The host wanted to know why. She wouldn't give her reason, but did say that her priorities had shifted over the years. Security was now much more important to her than stardom.

It soon became evident what she meant when the news appeared in *TV Guide* that she'd signed an unusually generous contract with Colson-Ames to play the role of a middle-aged matriarch on an as-yet-untitled daytime drama in preparation for WBS. Her decision elicited a certain amount of criticism for rejecting a costarring spot in primetime for the questionable honor of appearing in a lead on a soap opera in a part she was too young to play. Surprisingly, the usually acidulous Jess Brass rallied to her defense—"Give Florence McKinley credit for having the courage and foresight to deliberately choose a more challenging mature role when everyone's telling her to capitalize on her good looks while she's still got them."

The rumors began to circulate that the actress preferred more money to a bigger audience, that she was tightfisted and made extortionate demands of Colson-Ames, the producers of the new soap, "Riverday."

Maybe. It didn't surprise me that she might elect to take a chance on a soap instead of a sitcom, the longevity probability was greater for the former kind of program. And even if she *was* hard-nosed with respect to fiscal matters, hadn't more than a decade of shabby dressing rooms, low income, substandard fare, and the endless riding that comes with playing thin Broadway rejects in the heartland of America given her the right to cash in while she could? Suffering for the Muse appeals to adolescents, but winters are colder when you pass the three-decade marker and your circulation slows down.

Time vindicated her. The sitcom died unlamented after half a season. "Riverday" continues five days a week, fifty-two lucrative weeks a year.

I got out of my car and saw Lara standing in the doorway of the high old house, the porchlight silhouetting her against the darkness, her golden hair shimmering in and out of shadow.

I waved and started across the street. She walked down the long, narrow flight of stone steps leading from front door to pavement. I reached her when she was still a step above me. Our eyes met, she smiled and held out her hand and our fingertips too briefly brushed.

"Gene," she said, "I kept expecting you to call back and tell me you'd changed your mind. I wouldn't blame you if you did."

"No chance. Damsels in distress are my favorite hobby. Besides, I don't have Florence's number. Now what's this all about?"

"It's called calming down the star. I promised Ames she'd be in shape to tape tomorrow."

"Ames? Of Colson hyphen?"

"Yes. Colson is dead. Joseph T. Ames is our sole producer."

"Well, what's wrong with Florence? She still think someone is trying to frame her?"

"Yes."

"Anyone specific?"

"She won't say." Lara touched my arm lightly. "It's a nice night. Let's walk down to the end of the street and look at the river."

We descended to the sidewalk and strolled beneath the gentle glow of the streetlamps. Walking beside Lara, I thought of other summer nights when I was younger, watching couples walking quiet roads sharing secrets I wished I had the courage to fathom, telling myself it'd all be easier when I was older. But it never was.

"Hilary was right," Lara said as we neared the promenade. "The police came this morning and questioned everyone, especially Florence. By the time they were through with her, Flo was too upset to work, so our shooting schedule is now a mess, and that's one of the cardinal no-nos in our business."

"What makes her think she's being set up to take the blame for Niven's death?"

"She hasn't told me, Gene. Maybe she'll go into that with you. My job is just to get her relaxed enough so she can go to sleep and report tomorrow morning on set. Think you can help me with it?"

"I'll try. I still can't figure why me, though."

"Because you're the only detective I know. She wouldn't let me call someone from the Yellow Pages."

"What would you have done if we hadn't met? Get Hilary over here?"

"Hardly. Florence distrusts most other women on principle. She and Hilary have met, and neither much cared for the experience. Even when I told Florence about you, I had to pretend we'd been friends for years."

"I see now. I'm a desperation measure."

"You certainly are *not*. And please, love, I have enough temperament upstairs to deal with."

"I wasn't being serious. I was fishing for compliments."

She looked at me quizzically. "Ah? Such as?"

"Such as you called me because I've been on your mind. I've certainly been thinking about you."

"You shouldn't be." Said softly with her eyes averted, her hand touching my sleeve. Behind Lara, the clustered globes of lights across the water hung suspended in space. A boat mourned its passage from the river into Upper Bay and far down the walkway the strains of "Weeping Willow" lilted sadly through an open window. Near us on the promenade, arm in arm, a young couple dressed in faded jeans strolled in the semigloom, ignoring all scenery but each other. An old man with that vaguely familiar look often encountered in elderly indigents huddled forlornly on a bench with his back to the river and owlishly watched the winking saffron lights of Brooklyn Heights. Close to me, Lara's pupils glinted with the reflected glow of the distant shore. Her breath smelled sweet.

"Gene," she said, taking her hand away from my arm, "we'd better go inside."

She pushed the apartment door open and a fat tawny cat squeezed past and trotted into the hall. Lara put the key back in her pocket and smiled as the animal rubbed against my trouser legs. "That's Rathbone. If *he* accepts you, Florence probably will."

I shook Rathbone's paw and gently escorted him back into the apartment. Lara led me across a dark foyer to a large, disorderly, empty living room. "I'll go tell milady you're here." Lara left me alone to examine the chaos that was home to Florence McKinley.

Everywhere I turned I saw enormous clutter. Tattered manuscripts teetered precariously on two flimsy card tables, sheet music dangled from a black metal stand, one wall of bookshelves was mostly filled with dog-eared paperbacks and saddle-stapled Dramatists Play Service scripts. An old lace shawl hung neglectfully over the back of a dusty overstuffed gray sofa. LP albums—musicals, operas, masses, oratorios, spoken word discs and plays—lined one long baseboard; above them, innumerable stacked cassette cartridges barricaded a combination phonograph/FM/cassette tape recorder. Its dust cover was littered with loose file cards, a pen, a pair of scissors, a roll of Scotch tape and an FM program guide.

The machine was on. A cassette revolved within. From the speakers sounded the nervous scherzo of the Brahms piano trio in B, its vaguely sinister motif echoing again and again, fragmented and recombined by frenetic strings that filled the empty room with an air of ominous anticipation.

As my eyes ticked off the chamber's inventory in swift professional reconnaissance, I saw, in a corner by the great picture window overlooking promenade and river, the only neat, well-cared-for object in the place besides the cat: a gigantic aquarium, easily one hundred gallons capacity, fitted with a breathtaking miniaturization of a Medieval European village complete with shops, streets and a lofty mountain bridge leading to an ornate baronial manor carved with intricate detailing. But the diorama paled before the magnificence of the goldfish swimming in, around, past and through its nooks and recesses. A gorgeous profusion of colors, patterns, and shapes distinguished the many varieties . . . comets, ordinaries, fantails, nymphs, veiltails, calicos, shubunkins, and lionheads. One odd breed of piscine acrobat was brand-new to me. Its mode of navigation was so unusual it practically turned the creature into a living hoop. I bent over and squinted to see it more clearly.

"It's a tumbler, I had him imported. Please don't smear the glass."

I turned, startled that I hadn't heard the illustrious Florence McKinley enter the room.

I'd expected her to be distraught, but she was putting on a good act of being in control. Tall, cool, aloof, she was slim and sleek in a long tan at-home robe that draped her slender figure and fell nearly to the floor, stopping just above tiny feet encased in white slippers. She extended her hand to me, smiling distantly, a queen acknowledging the presence of an ardent commoner. Damned if I didn't fall into the expected role and raise her fingers to my lips.

She had the poise and containment of a fashion model. Her brown hair was carefully arranged in an upswept mass of curls, no strand out of place. Dark steady eyes. Her crimson lips, full and slightly parted, had a gloss that diverted my attention from her heavily rouged cheeks. She had Kate Hepburn bone structure and all the planes of her face tapered down to a firm chin unparenthesized by jowls. On first glance, she seemed as I remembered her . . . the glamorous Florence McKinley of early television rather than the homey Martha Jennett of "Riverday." But as my gaze lingered on her features, my eyes saw more than I wanted: the base coat minimizing tiny lines puckering the skin at her temples, the gray lusterless hair near the roots, the mottling that small blue veins worked beneath her eyes and at the tip of her nose.

Yet it was still an arresting face, scored but not yet effaced by time. Her eyes held mine, studying and evaluating what they saw. Looking down, she noticed her tubby cat rubbing against my legs. She smiled more warmly than before.

"A man who likes goldfish and is liked, in turn, by Rathbone has much to recommend him. Rathbone is very choosy about the company he keeps. Come, sit and talk to me." She sat on the sofa and patted the cushion next to her. I did as she bid and Lara chose an armchair across from us, an overstuffed green affair that threatened to envelop her like an amoeba.

We passed a few moments in obligatory politeness. I reinforced the fiction that Lara and I had known each other for years. Our host's arch looks implied our friendship was more than casual, or was so once.

We talked of felines and fish. She said her aquarium cost $450 used, her tumbler ran close to $200 new, that she bought all her accessories in lower Manhattan, that her cat adopted her in Indiana while she played a supporting role in a touring version of Ouida Rathbone's unjustly obscure *Sherlock Holmes*, written especially for her husband, Basil.

Lara glanced at her watch more than once. As soon as I could, I brought up the problem of Ed Niven's death. Florence McKinley's animation immediately disappeared. Her shoulders slumped, her flood of chatter ebbed away, her pale hands stopped in midgesture and came to rest on her lap. She looked down dully at them. I realized the poise she'd put on to greet me was all pose.

"I'm sorry I'm going to have to ask things you must have had to deal with this morning, but it's absolutely essential I know at least as much as the police if I'm going to be of any use."

She nodded. "Go ahead. First question?"

"Where were you when Niven fell?"

"Here. At home."

"Can you prove it?"

"No."

"Think hard. Did you leave your house at any time Saturday? Could a neighbor, a local shopkeeper testify you were in the vicinity?"

She shook her head. "Lately, I've had more than the usual number of script pages to learn, they've been using me quite heavily on the show. Saturday I was busy all day with my part. I never left the apartment."

"Then you have no alibi." I turned up one palm. "The next question, I'm afraid, has to be whether you and Mr. Niven recently quarreled over anything?"

"All lovers do." Even subdued, her voice had that familiar vibrancy that impressionists sometimes parodied. I could imagine her singing opera in the shower and sounding pretty good.

"Any special argument I ought to know about?"

"No."

I doubted that, but figured if it was important enough, I'd hear about it eventually, maybe from Lara. I went on to the next point. "Do you have any notion, Ms. McKinley, what Mr. Niven was doing at the studio on his day off?"

She shrugged, avoiding my eyes. "He kept all his writing materials at WBS. He rarely worked at home."

"But isn't there another possibility?"

"What?"

"That he went to the studio to meet someone?"

"*No.*" Declared with such passion I think it surprised her almost as much as me. Just then, the Brahms trio ended and she used it as a convenient circumstance to occupy herself with the dials.

"Excuse me, I was recording off the air," she said, returning to the sofa a moment later. "Now what did you ask?"

"Whether Mr. Niven might have had an appointment Saturday."

"Yes, of course it's possible. I shouldn't have been so quick to reply without thinking. But he told me he'd be busy all weekend."

"Doing what?"

Instead of answering, she turned to Lara and asked whether she'd mind going to the kitchen to make some tea. Lara said she'd be glad to and looked anything but. After she was gone, my host, putting her finger to her lips, rose and softly glided across the carpet to the entryway. Only after she'd called down the hall and got a distant answer from Lara, presumably in the kitchen, did Florence nod in satisfaction and sit back down beside me.

"Excuse me for acting so mysterious," she said, "but sweet as she is, Lara is not the soul of discretion at all times."

"How do you mean?"

She shook her head, smiling.

"No, no, that's neither here nor there. The important thing is that I could not discuss what you'd asked with her in the room. Or anyone else from the cast, for that matter. You want to know what Eddie was presumably preoccupied with this past weekend?"

"That's right."

"Well, it had to do with the new 'Riverday' 'Bible.' Do you know what I'm talking about?"

"Sure. Has nothing to do with evangelism. The 'Bible' is the long-range plot synopsis of a soap opera, right?"

"Yes. Eddie told me he'd be working on his latest one this weekend. I didn't want to alarm Lara. Cast members aren't supposed to know about it."

"But why would it alarm her?"

"Because he is . . . was quite overdue in preparing it.

He was supposed to turn in a draft of the 'Bible' by the beginning of this week."

"How bad does that leave off 'Riverday'?"

"It's not good," she replied grimly. "If we don't get a new head writer fast, pretty soon it will be improvisation time for the cast."

She brooded on it for a moment. I asked her how come she knew so much about the "Bible" if cast members are supposed to be kept in the dark about it. It was the absolute thousand percent wrong question. It provoked a filibuster on the way youth was exploited on TV to the detriment of maturer talent. I listened, puzzled, as "Mother Jennett" denounced producers, the network, sponsors, most of all her "loyal fans."

"The fickle bastards want your soul along with your autograph, but catch *me* giving perfect strangers the means to forge my signature!" In her agitation, she rose and stalked about the room, her swirling robes accidentally sweeping the program guide, scissors and Scotch tape off the phonograph dust cover onto the floor. She picked them up and replaced them. Seemingly calmer, she turned to me.

"Lara said you watch 'Riverday.'"

"That's right."

"Do you remember Kit Yerby?"

"I ought to. She was on Friday's episode."

"Well, that was practically the last time you'll see her. Snippy little bitch, got arrested once for shoplifting, but that's neither here nor there. Our ratings slipped two points last month and she happened to be up for contract renewal. They fired her so they could budget some young stud that the fat ladies in Duluth will doubtlessly drool over."

Why did she sound so grimly satisfied about it? I was going to ask her when an altogether different question popped into my mind. It wasn't important to anyone but me, but I asked it, anyway.

"Does this so-called stud happen to be named Harry Whelan?"

"Yes. I think so. You know him?"

"Unfortunately."

"Oh? Thereon, I believe, hangs a tale."

"Irrelevant. Let's get back to the original question."

"I forget what it was."

"How you happen to know so much about Ed Niven's 'Bible.'"

"Oh. Yes." She sat back down. "Years ago, when Joe Ames originally called to offer me the part of Martha Jennett, I knew all the risks involved. I told him if I took it, I'd be the first Emmy winner to turn down primetime for a soap opera and would expect certain concessions in return for the publicity that would bring. He argued a bit, but that was only a matter of form. He eventually agreed to most of my terms. One was that I see every new 'Bible' as soon as it's written."

"They gave you story approval?" An unheard-of thing. "I'm impressed."

"Not quite. Officially, all I'm entitled to is a copy of every updated synopsis." Her lips curved ironically. "But you know what they say about a little knowledge."

"So that's what Niven was supposed to be busy with this weekend, writing a new 'Bible.' The old one's practically used up?"

"Yes." She muttered something about ratings taking a suicidal plunge. "But not this week. His death will attract the vultures."

"Will Ames promote your other writer?"

"Tommy Franklin?" She grimaced. "Extremely improbable."

"Why?"

"His plotting ideas are idiotic."

"Oh? Can you give me an example?"

But just then Lara interrupted by putting her head into the room to say that tea was ready. Florence nodded, and the blonde entered with a small tray bearing three cups, saucers, a china pot and nothing else. I was disappointed. I'd hoped for something to eat, even a few cookies would have been pleasant.

"We're almost done," I told Lara. "Ms. McKinley, I don't like to distress you, but is there any chance Mr. Niven told you he'd be working this weekend so that he could meet someone else?"

She raised her cup and sipped. "By someone else, you're implying that there might be another woman?"

"Yes."

"It may be true." Her lips curved downward in a sour frown. "Over the past few months, Eddie canceled several dates with me." She stared into her cup as if reading secrets in the leaves. "And now you know what we quarreled about."

"Assuming there is another woman involved, have you any idea who it might be?"

She exchanged a glance with Lara before saying she wasn't sure. That annoyed me, but I made a note to ask Lara later. "All right," I continued, "you told Lara you think someone is trying to make it look like you were responsible for Mr. Niven's death. Is that person the woman you have in mind?"

"I didn't say I had anyone particular in mind."

"You're fencing with me. Is the reason you won't name her because she's also an actress on 'Riverday'?"

I got another noncommittal answer. My temper was rising. It was almost ten o'clock, I was hungry and tired and still had a two-hour trip home.

"Look," I complained, "you're holding back information wholesale. If you don't trust me enough to speak your mind freely, there's no point in continuing. I can't accept you as my client unless—"

"At this stage," she broke in, "I neither trust nor distrust you. You're here on your lady's recommendation. I am not your client till *I* say so . . . you haven't even told me yet what you charge!" She emphasized the last word with a smart tap on my knee with her forefinger.

I put down my cup and rose to my feet. But my eyes connected with Lara's and her mute "please" stopped me from walking out. *Ah, damn,* I thought, if I could put up with Hilary treating me like chattel (as I had for several years), I supposed I could tolerate a bit more of the same for her cousin's sake.

"Okay," I told McKinley, swallowing my indignation, my pride and my tea, "will you at least tell me why you think you *are* a target?" I sat down again.

"Yes." Though there were just the three of us in the apartment, she lowered her voice to a melodramatic whisper. "This morning, I found something in my dressing room."

"What?"

"A pile of Eddie's clothing."

Not good. I asked her to reconstruct the moment. She closed her eyes and re-created it in her mind. As she did, her fingers trailed along her cheek in concentration. "A quarter past six. The door was slightly ajar. That bothered me immediately, I always keep it locked. I pushed it open, switched on the light. First thing I saw was a pair of men's shoes under my makeup table. I checked the label. 7½ triple Es."

"Niven's size?"

"Yes. He used to complain how hard it was to find stylish shoes that fit."

"What did you do when you found them?"

"I had a bad feeling about it. I started opening dresser drawers and, sure enough, stuck in the back of one was a bloody shirt of his that I recognized, along with trousers, socks and underwear, all crumpled up."

"Did you show the clothing to the police?"

"No. I got rid of them."

"You did *what?*"

Her eyes snapped open. "Don't bark at me. I was frightened. I knew I had no alibi for Saturday. I didn't want the police to find the clothes in my room."

"*How* did you get rid of them?"

"It's not important."

It took all the reserve I had not to call her a string of names. Instead, I merely pointed out that what she'd done might be viewed as an obstruction of justice, maybe worse. Then I really zinged her. "Has it occurred to you that the police already may know the clothing was in your dressing room?"

"How could they?"

"You can bet they searched the studio from roof to basement. What makes you imagine a team of professionals would miss something you saw immediately?"

"They told the public—"

"Just what they intend the public to know, nothing more. Maybe they wanted to see what you'd do with the clothing."

"Oh, God!" Her face went white. She raised her hands histrionically and pressed knuckles to temples, wincing. "*Oh, my God!*" It was not her most impressive performance.

Up to then, Lara hadn't said a word, but now she stood up and asked me to join her in the hall. McKinley was too caught up in her private *angst* to object.

I followed Lara into the corridor. When we were out of

earshot, she turned so suddenly I almost bumped into her. "Gene," she snapped, "I asked you to help me calm her down. You're upsetting her worse than ever."

"Look, this whole business is poison. I can lose my license if I don't report what she did with his clothes."

"*Surely* you won't get in any trouble if you don't report it tonight?" In her anger, her resemblance to Hilary was more pronounced than ever.

"I'd love to let it rest. I'm worn out, and hungry as hell."

Her manner softened at once. "Why? Didn't you eat?"

"I didn't have time. After you called, I showered and shaved and hopped in the car."

"Poor baby!" She touched my cheek gently. "All to please Hilary's cousin."

"Correction—as a favor to you."

"All right, let me atone. Say something comforting to Florence, then come home with me and I'll fix you a light supper."

The stuff of fantasy . . . a quiet tête-à-tête with a dream girl. Except I couldn't. "Lara, that's the best offer I've had all month, but I've still got to drive back to Philly tonight."

"Absolutely not. I won't hear of it, I can see you're exhausted. If you had an accident on the road, I'd never forgive myself. And neither would Hilary."

"But—"

"Hush, no arguments! You can use my sofa bed."

I tried to convince myself that going home with Lara would solve nothing, but at that moment, my common sense decided to take a leave of absence.

I eased Florence's mind on the subject of the police knowing about the clothes. No talk now about what I'd charge, she insisted I take her on as my client. I hedged on committing myself, but promised I'd at least look into the matter on her behalf.

"One condition, though . . . I want to see your dressing room immediately."

"Tomorrow morning?"

"The sooner the better. And while I'm there, I need to ask a few discreet questions around the studio."

"I'll make arrangements so you can," Florence assured me, suddenly seized with the spirit of cooperation.

I waited at the hall entry while Lara fussed over her friend, plumping up the pillows of the armchair nearest the aquarium, turning off the air pump for the night—presumably to save Florence a few pennies in electricity—tuning in WQXR, bringing her enough Valium to sedate a horse.

"That's how she gets ready for bed," Lara explained. We said good night and left Florence McKinley staring peacefully at her fish while the strains of "The Perfect Fool" played over her FM.

Starlight and champagne can't hide an insult to the stomach. I'm quoting Hilary. A lot of men would have been glaucous with envy at the prospect of my late supper with Lara in her Riverside Drive penthouse, but the reality of thawed quiche, wilted salad and stale croissants only would have been marginally palatable if washed down with large drafts of Veuve Clicquot or at the very least, a few pints of Watney's Red Barrel.

I got mineral water, uncarbonated.

Lara's apartment was lofty and slightly sumptuous. Florid floral arrangements graced polished mahogany bureaus, hand-woven straw placemats held down with sparkling silver service rested on a great curved glass dining table. Delicate crystal figurines danced motionless in carved shadow boxes on textured-paper walls that matched the deep-pile carpeting. The obligatory actor's stock-in-trade of Stanislavski, Herman, Spolin, Corson and innumerable softcover playscripts filled the shelves of a tall lacquered oriental bookcase next to a beige armchair adjacent to a Lucite magazine caddy neatly stuffed with the latest numbers of *Cosmopolitan, Vogue, Glamour, People, Variety* and *Back Stage*. In the foyer, beside a pink-and-gold designer telephone placed on a butterfly-shaped end table, I saw the most recent issue of *Ross Reports*, the TV industry's indispensable monthly update of the whereabouts of all major producers, casting personnel and talent agents.

Admittedly, interior design isn't my long suit. I suppose my tastes are still small-town Ohio, but Lara's glossy, sleek apartment reminded me too much of one of those never-been-lived-in model rooms you see in the furniture department at Gimbel's.

I nibbled at my feast as Lara nervously chatted about anything that occurred to her. She seemed determined to mention Hilary's name at least once every minute. Her eyes kept glancing away from mine. When I was done eating, she asked me what I thought about her friend Florence's predicament. Leaving the table, I chose the beige chair near the bookcase and sat down.

"Well, she's in a jam," I conceded. "How bad I can't say. If she'd tell me the truth—"

Lara frowned. "You think she's lying?"

"She's certainly holding back information. Like the name of the woman she thinks Niven was seeing on the side. And what she did with his clothing. And why she thinks she's being set up."

"Surely," Lara interposed with a flip of her hand, "that's because she feels the mysterious woman deliberately put the clothing in her room."

"But there's a two-way discrepancy. Number one—why didn't the police find the garments if they've been there all weekend?"

"You told Flo they might've been left there by the inspector to trap her."

"I said that to rattle her into divulging what she did with them. Lou Betterman's style isn't subtlety. If he suspected her, he would have hit her with it when he questioned everybody this morning at the studio."

"So you don't think the police *are* watching Florence?"

Her inflection made me look up. "Why?"

"This afternoon she thought someone was spying on her."

"Where? When?"

"Outside her house in Brooklyn Heights. I rode there with Florence in the limo. We went straight from the studio. On the way up the front steps, she turned around and claimed there was a man in a dark coat watching her."

"Did you see anyone?"

"No. When I turned, she said he'd concealed himself in a doorway across the street. I couldn't spot him, though."

"Maybe," I suggested drily, "it was one of Florence's loyal fans."

The ghost of a smirk on Lara's lips. "All right, what's the other discrepancy that makes you think she wasn't telling the truth about finding the clothes this morning?"

"Presumably," I said, "discovering his things frightened Florence into thinking they were planted deliberately to cast suspicion on her. Isn't that the impression she gave you?"

"Yes."

"Well, if that's the case—and if she really *did* find the clothing early this morning—how come she already thought someone was trying to frame her *yesterday* afternoon?"

Lara's forehead furrowed, then she realized what I meant. "My God, she told me that on the phone when I called her long distance from your place!"

"Exactly. Roughly fourteen hours before she allegedly saw his 7½ triple Es beneath her makeup table."

We pondered it, but came up with nothing of any particular value. Lara brushed aside a strand of silky hair from her eyes, put her chin in her hand and regarded me thoughtfully.

"A penny?" I suggested.

"You know, Gene, I have a good idea who this hypothetical other woman is. Want to exchange secrets?"

"Hmm?"

"I'm curious what Flo thought so important she had to send me out of the room to tell you."

"Sorry, Lara, that's privileged information."

"Then I suppose it has something to do with the 'Riverday' 'Bible.'"

I tried to act casual, but Lara laughed and as she did, a deep dimple appeared in her left cheek, the mirror image of Hilary's. "Better take acting lessons, love, you don't exactly have a poker face."

"Why do you think we were discussing the 'Bible'?"

"The context just before she hustled me into the kitchen. It's a commonly known fact she holds plenty of behind-the-scenes clout when it comes to the developing storyline. If Flo takes a disliking to a new actor, chances are the character she plays will catch a fatal disease just before her contract comes up for reoption."

"Which suggests another line of speculation," I said. "How did Florence feel about Kit Yerby? She said she was fired recently."

"True. And Flo didn't like her, Kit was too friendly with Ed. Or tried to be."

"So you think Florence suspects her?"

"I'd say no. Ed didn't encourage Kit. But on the other hand, Kit was written out rather abruptly."

"Meaning?"

"Meaning Florence may have had her fired."

"How could she do that?"

"A star has a lot of clout, Gene," Lara explained. "And Florence loves to dig up interesting little facts about everyone she can, just in case she needs extra leverage with Ames. I'm probably the only person in the entire cast she doesn't keep a file on or talk about behind my back."

"I wouldn't bet on that," I remarked drily. "When you were out of the room, she couldn't resist a little slap at you, either."

"Oh?"

"According to our dear Ms. McKinley, you are not the soul of discretion."

Lara suddenly yawned. "Excuse me, Gene. I've had about enough of Flo's neurotic friendship for one evening. It's getting close to my bedtime."

"Spare just one more minute, okay?"

"Okay."

"Might Kit Yerby have blamed Ed for losing her role?"

"Enough to push him off a roof?" She gave me a sardonic smile. "Gene, normal soap actors don't go crazy when they're written out. It happens too often, a normal business risk. Kit's agent already got her on another show . . . in fact, Ed helped arrange it."

"I see. Then who *do* you think Florence's other woman is?"

"No question about it, Gene, it's Joanne Carpenter. She and Flo hate each other."

"Why?"

"The story is that Flo took Ed away from Joanne a long time ago." She put her hand over her mouth and yawned again. "Gene, I've really got to get some sleep. The limo arrives early."

I followed her to the linen closet and she handed me bed things. I would have kissed her good night, but Lara backed off and I found myself two inches from her cheek. We agreed on an arm's-length handshake, but I could have sworn she felt the same as I did at that moment.

"Sleep well, love," Lara murmured, then hurried to her room.

1:45 A.M. The apartment was dark except for the dim amber glow of a digital alarm clock near me. Through filmy window curtains I saw the cool light of remote stars beckoning me to a party I could never attend.

I couldn't sleep. The hardness of the sofa bed did not place my spine in a state of grace. Yet in the past I've tolerated army cots and sleeping bags. It was my brain that refused to switch off. Unanswerable questions played tag in my head, repeating over and over again like an endless loop of tape. I tried to lull myself by meditating on the subtle variances of Hilary's and Lara's faces, but that was not conducive to rest. I cast about for another topic and hit upon Joanne Carpenter, Florence's supposed Nemesis.

Joanne was one of the few remaining cast members of "Riverday's" original lineup of actors. She portrayed Eloise Savage, a semivillainous manipulator of securities and lives who loved power almost as much as she longed for Dr. Matt Jennett, older brother of Roberta, played by Lara—

Why was it so hard to get her out of my mind? It was more than mere libido. The ghost of an idea almost surfaced, only to be exorcised by the recollection of Lara's frank, appraising smile.

Damn.

I concentrated with renewed determination on Joanne Carpenter, re-creating in my mind's eye her physical appearance as she last looked on "Riverday": thin, graceful, smartly dressed in a kelly green suit that complemented her copper hair and hazel eyes. Her low-drooping lids— rather reminiscent of Lauren Bacall's—made her appear slightly dissipated. And very sexy.

I mused on my oversusceptibility to women's eyes. I see too much in them. Hilary's alleged vulnerability, masked by flint. The frightened waif deep within Florence McKinley who assumed regal airs and lied with that guileless innocence actors share with children. *But what if she's really a cobra?*

Lara—*thinking about her again*—was different, at least. Her eyes were direct and frank and if they said things she wasn't ready to act upon, that was her prerogative as a woman, I supposed. At least she didn't look at me as if she wanted to make me over in her father's image.

I told myself I was being as foolish about her as I'd been in the past over Hilary. Too quick to equate good character with good looks. Obliterating reality instead of relishing its blemishes. *A subtler sort of sexism.*

A feeble ray of light stole across the living room as I lay in darkness. Sitting up like the old man in a Poe story, I saw Lara standing in the chiaroscuro created by the lamplight spilling through her bedroom door. The glow penetrated her filmy gown.

"Gene?" She uttered my name so softly I wasn't certain whether it was the sound or the thought I heard.

"Yes?" I also spoke in a low voice.

"Have you been able to sleep?"

"No."

"I can't, either."

Silence. Neither of us moved. I gazed longingly at her lithe body silhouetted in the suffused aura of the lamplight. Her breasts rose and fell in the same rhythm as my pulse. The room was a lagoon of darkness and pale flame. Its midnight waters lapped us both.

When Lara finally drew near, I rose and rested my

hands gently on her shoulders, smelling the delicate fragrance of her smooth skin.

"We're practically strangers," she whispered. "We're acting out a fantasy, aren't we?"

"I think so."

"I've played too many scenes like this, Gene. The characters always suffer. I don't want to get hurt."

"I could promise you it'll never happen, but we both know that's not how love works."

"Is this love?"

"It feels similar."

"It usually does at first."

Afraid to continue, unable to stop, we held each other for a long while, but when my lips touched hers, Lara responded at first, then abruptly pulled away.

"You're kissing Hilary, not me."

"That's not true."

"Isn't it? Be honest."

"I don't think so. I can't be positive."

"Neither can I." She stood inches and miles away. "God, Gene, this is so complicated."

"It doesn't have to be."

"Show me how to make it simple."

"Just make up your mind whether you want to stay with me or not."

"That's the trouble, love. I'm not sure."

I helped her decide.

Just before dawn, Lara fell asleep in my arms. Gazing down on her exquisite features, so like and unlike Hilary's, I tried to believe in the incredible fact that I was holding the very woman I'd watched month after adoring month on my TV screen. But it was a marvel beyond my comprehension, perhaps because the creature whose head I cradled was so vastly different from Roberta Jennett, the fiercely independent woman she played on "Riverday."

As the hush of twilight muffled the city, I began to doze, too. Bits of phrases, scraps of logic and music lulled me as the faint flush of morning crept through the thin curtains and warmed my closed eyelids.

The alarm was as shrill and startling as if someone had splashed ice water on me, cubes and all. I bolted straight up as Lara reached over and shut off the clock.

Every new romance has tricky moments when the bond so recently formed either holds fast or begins to fray. We were facing our first crucial test: waking up together, feeling oddly shy and vulnerable. There was such an equivocal expression on Lara's face that I suddenly was afraid to say or do anything, lest it inadvertently hurt her. She tried to smile, but her eyes glistened, and she pulled the covers to her chin with an after-the-fact modesty that was both poignant and endearing.

No longer tongue-tied, I put my hand reassuringly over hers. "Lainie?"

"What?" she whispered.

"Remember what I said last night? About love?"

Lara nodded, eyes wide with uncertainty.

"The similarity's growing," I said.

First she smiled.

We had to hurry. I did what I could to make myself presentable, but without fresh clothing or toiletry articles, it was a haphazard job. Lara loaned me the razor she used on her legs, and I managed to shave without cutting myself more than one or two thousand times, but at least there was styptic.

The studio limo picked us up in front of the building Lara lived in. The driver followed West End all the way down to Fifty-third. It was so early, there was hardly any traffic. We were the only passengers, a minor mercy, considering that my metabolism wasn't yet aware I was supposed to be awake.

The car pulled up in front of an ugly gray concrete monolith on the north side of Fifty-third. The Hudson glinting in the distance was the only sparkling sight in an otherwise dingy neighborhood. Ramshackle hovels squeezing together on the south side of the street were crowded by greasy warehouses and garages. I wouldn't walk there at night, and even broad daylight didn't much appeal to me.

As we disembarked, a fat young man with a camera slung round his neck hurried over to us and got Lara's permission to photograph the two of us together. I was stunned that even the most rabid fan would hang around that forbidding block so early in the morning. Lara signed his autograph book, then handed it to me with a wink. I scribbled in it, too, figuring, what the hell, he probably had no idea who Tom Mason was.

Lara steered me to the front entrance of the squat network building. It resembled a stone fortress or prison: grim, bleak, few windows and all of them streaked with grime.

"Once," Lara told me, "this was the biggest production facility in the East. Some of the 'golden age' dramatic series were broadcast from here. Then TV went west, and this became the biggest white elephant in the East—at least until WBS bought it."

"And now the only things they use this gothic horror for are 'Riverday' and the news?"

"And for storage and general administrative space. Maybe as a partial tax writeoff, I don't know—though the revenues they get for 'Riverday' are astronomical."

I opened the lobby door. We entered a commonplace reception area devoid of any furniture other than one long bench and a desk behind which sat a burly, red-faced security guard in his late twenties. Lara signed a list he pushed across his desk, and motioned for me to do the same.

Taking back the list, the guard asked me for identification. As I pulled out my driver's license, he flipped through a separate sheaf of papers but was unable to find my name anywhere.

I explained that I'd been invited by Florence McKinley. He shook his head and shrugged apologetically.

"I'm sorry, but I've got nothing here to clear you." His voice was as musical as someone gargling with gravel.

Lara stepped forward. "Hasn't Ms. McKinley arrived yet?" He said no. "Never mind, this man's with me, you can pass him in on my say-so."

"Sorry, ma'am, I can't. Gotta be okayed by WBS or Mr. Ames."

"Since when?"

"Since that turkey jumped off the roof."

Lara reddened, but I stopped her from arguing. "You

go in," I suggested, "I'll wait out here for Florence to arrive."

"That could be a while yet, Gene, she's not on till the fourth scene. All right, look—you stay here, I'll run on up and get Micki to clear you." Without explaining who Micki was, Lara exited through an iron door to the left of and behind the security desk.

The guard mopped his florid face. "Guess I'll catch hell for not taking her word you're okay," he said morosely, "but they already fired another guard for Saturday, and he only had one year left to retirement."

"I'm not mad," I said. "I understand the position you're in, I used to be a security guard myself once."

"Yeah? Where'd you work? What kinda place?"

"A bank."

"You had it easy," he rasped wryly. "Money at least stays put. It don't rob itself."

Micki turned out to be Marianne Lipscomb, assistant to the producer of "Riverday." A tiny brunette with hair parted in the middle and swept over her ears in two midnight wings. Her small oval face had large brown eyes and a nose that overbalanced everything else. Likewise, her trim frame looked lopsided because her shoulders were too broad. But she had so much poise she looked like she knew exactly what she was going to be doing for the next thirteen weeks, minute by minute, and maybe she did.

Emerging from the same door Lara left by, Micki Lipscomb introduced herself to me, then rounded on the guard. He started to argue with her, but gave up after a few acrimonious exchanges, during which she impressed on him that her authorization was synonymous with that of Joseph T. Ames himself.

I was finally permitted behind the metal door. Ames'

assistant led me through a maze of corridors studded
with so many unnumbered doors I felt like the lost child
in George Macdonald's fairy tale about goblins. Heeltap-
ping briskly in front, Micki took me up two flights of
steep stairs to the third-floor offices of Colson-Ames.

I entered a suite of cramped cubicles opening off a
moderately large central space filled with phones, desks,
chairs, filing cabinets and a barrage of color TV sets.

"Wait here," she instructed me. "I can't let you into the
studio without direct clearance from Mr. Ames, and I can
assure you he won't give it to you unless Florence tells
him to." She took a deep breath. "Did she ask you here
because of what happened to Ed Niven?"

"Yes. Did you know him very well?"

She cocked an eyebrow. "You might put it that way."

I regarded her curiously. *Another candidate?* "I heard
he was dating Ms. McKinley."

"What a quaint phrase," she said ironically. "I didn't
know that people still 'date' nowadays."

"Some of us do. I also understand Mr. Niven used to be
involved with Joanne Carpenter."

"If you're going to dredge up ancient history, you're
going to need a score card. Ed 'dated' anything with two
sets of curves. I *think* he drew the line at nymphets." Her
lips seemed unsure whether to frown or sneer. Just then
the phone rescued her from deciding.

She held the receiver to her ear for a few seconds, then
hung up and strode over to her desk. "That was Mr.
Ames. Emergency meeting on set. You'll have to keep
yourself company for a while." Marianne Lipscomb
grabbed a clipboard and pencil and hurried out.

Some detectives I've met regard an empty office as an
invitation to poke around in drawers and files, but since I
had no idea what I might be looking for, I reserved the
temptation for a time when it might be worth the risk. I

busied myself, instead, reading the cartoons, memos and interoffice dictums pinned to the bulletin board. One of the latter was an emphatic note from Joseph T. Ames warning cast members that costumes "are the property of Colson-Ames and MUST BE RETURNED TO WARD-ROBE IMMEDIATELY after taping is done, SOONER if possible so they can be cleaned ASAP. Costumes will NOT be loaned for personal use under any circumstances, and may only be worn in public at publicity functions approved by ME!" Next to this directive someone had pinned up a caricature of an elderly white-haired man, presumably a likeness of Ames, sneaking out of the wardrobe department wearing an evening gown and huge earrings.

The bulletin board also held several yellowing lists of union rules and restrictions, a few fan letters, and a note on NBC stationery challenging the "Riverday" company to a softball match with the cast and crew of "Another World." There was also a scene-by-scene breakdown of the day's taping run with space on it for the actors to initial upon arrival. The place beside Florence's name was blank, as was Joanne Carpenter's, but neither were involved in the first scenes on the schedule.

Most of the memos were soiled and wrinkled with age, but one notice on the middle of the board was new. As I read it, I started to understand what the lobby officer meant about money being easier to guard than the stars he was responsible for.

WBS Memorandum
8/17

To: ALL PEOPLE IN THE 53rd STREET FACIL-ITY

From: PAUL C. BAUER, MANAGER, SECURITY

BECAUSE OF THIS WEEKEND'S TRAGEDY, NO ONE WILL BE PERMITTED IN THE FA-

CILITY AFTER HOURS WITHOUT PERMIS-
SION FROM THE NETWORK OR AN AUTHO-
RIZED PRODUCER. PLEASE DO NOT TRY
TO "BEAT THE SYSTEM." WHENEVER YOU
DO, YOU ENDANGER LIVES AND PROPER-
TIES. I HAVE REPEATEDLY ASKED ACTORS
AND TECHNICIANS TO OBSERVE THE FOL-
LOWING SAFETY MEASURES:

1. Use the front doors to enter and exit. The fire
   doors are for emergencies only and MUST NOT
   BE PROPPED OPEN WHEN YOU GO OUT TO
   LUNCH.

2. Lock your dressing room at all times, even if you
   are inside, and especially when changing clothes.
   NEVER LEAVE YOUR ROOM KEYS IN THE
   DOOR!

3. If you see someone suspicious on the premises,
   avoid confronting the transgressor. Report his or
   her presence IMMEDIATELY to Security.

Thank you.

The puzzle in my mind now had another piece that fit.
There was no record of Niven signing in at the front desk
Saturday, so he must have entered through a fire door.
Someone in the building may have left one open for him
deliberately, or it may have been ajar by pure chance,
but it seemed the only way Niven could have gotten in.

And whoever pushed him must have left the same way.

Along one wall of the production office there were several TV sets arranged in two banks, one above the other.
Some were tuned to the on-air programs being broadcast
by WBS and its three rival networks. Others were studio
monitors that showed familiar "Riverday" sets, some of
the same ones that the taping breakdown on the bulletin
board specified for use that day. On one screen I saw the

Jennett family's living room, on another the hospital room where various characters had, from time to time, recuperated under the affectionate eye of Dr. Matt Jennett. Another monitor was of the supper club owned by Martha and her husband, Leo Jennett (Florence McKinley and Donald Bannister, respectively).

As I watched, technicians wandered in and out of scenes, checking props, adjusting furniture, dusting bureau and desk tops. A chubby young woman in jeans fussed with the hospital bed, arranged props on the adjacent nightstand—water tray, a box of tissues, a medicine bottle and dosage cup about the size and shape of a shot glass. A flurry of movement in the Jennett living room caught my eye. I focused on that monitor.

The efficient Ms. Lipscomb appeared on the screen, still holding her clipboard. She was saying something to a tall, white-haired man in his sixties with a dour hangdog expression drawing down the corners of his mouth as if he were smelling a rotten egg. He wore no tie, but had on a gray flannel suit he must have been roasting in. Clearly the original of the man in drag caricatured on the bulletin board, I assumed (correctly as it turned out) that he was Joseph T. Ames, the producer.

A group of familiar people drifted on the set and sat down on the armchairs and lounges. I recognized platinum-haired VeldaLee Royce, who played the eldest Jennett daughter, Bella. On the show, Bella was nine months pregnant, but VeldaLee must have delivered over the weekend; her tummy was flat and her waist wasp-thin. Ira Powell—the actor who plays her brother, Matt—flopped onto the right end of a sofa and put his head in his hands. He didn't look well.

The other end of the sofa was occupied by Donald Bannister, the veteran thespian who portrayed Leo "Father" Jennett.

Lara, twice as beautiful as recent memory served, look-

ing rounder than she was in truth (for the TV camera adds
ten pounds to a performer's apparent weight), started to
sit between the two men on the sofa. Pausing, she made a
face and moved over to perch on the arm of the couch
next to her make-believe daddy, Donald Bannister, and
as far away as possible from Ira "Matt" Powell.

Ames began to harangue the assembled cast members.
Gesticulating with wildly flailing arms, he occasionally
flung a remark to Micki Lipscomb, who scribbled on her
notepad with head ducking up and down like a novelty-
store plastic bird whose beak eternally dips into brackish
water.

I wanted to hear what was being said in the Jennett
living room, but there was no audio. I reached for the
volume control, but the set was one of the upper ones
and the sound knob was just beyond my grasp.

"Leave it alone," a sardonic voice said behind me.
"He's not worth listening to."

I turned and saw a woman signing the taping schedule
on the bulletin board. I had to look carefully to make
sure it was Joanne Carpenter. On the show, as Eloise Savage, she was always impeccably coiffed, expensively and
excellently groomed, but the real Joanne Carpenter was
casual to the point of disarray. Her copper hair hung lank
and languid on either side of unrouged cheeks. No lipstick, no shadow above eyes that gaped myopically from
behind thick rimless glasses. She wore patched and tattered faded jeans and a rumpled orange T-shirt bearing
the legend, "The more I know men, the more I love my
dog."

Smiling uncertainly, she extended her hand and shook
mine. "Don't tell me, let me guess, you're the new head
writer?"

"No, sorry." I introduced myself by name and profession.

"Really? I've never met a detective. Where's your

gun?" She seemed disappointed when I said I wasn't carrying one. "Are you here because of what happened to Ed Niven?"

"Yes."

"I'd like to help any way I can. Ed and I used to be good friends. If I can do anything, please feel free to ask." She said it with great earnestness, but I had to remind myself that she, like Florence, made a living out of pretense.

"Thanks, Ms. Carpenter, I *would* like to talk with you." I gestured toward the monitor. "But don't you have to go to that meeting?"

She smiled. "Now how can I be there if no one told me about it?" A vigorous toss of her head. "I believe I'm going to pass up a chance to hear the usual Joe Ames 'ratings are slipping' sermon and go straight up to Makeup. Want to come with me?"

"I'd better not. I'm not authorized."

"Oh, hell," she scoffed, "I'll be responsible."

I shook my head, pointing to the notice from the WBS security chief. She stood close to the board, read it, then turned and shrugged. "Sorry, I didn't know. I was off yesterday."

Florence entered the office. "Never mind, Joanna, dear, *I'll* be responsible for him." Brushing past her, she came over and took my arm.

"Darling," Florence purred, "aren't you on in the fourth scene?"

"Yes," Joanne replied curtly. "So what?"

"Don't you think you'd better toddle on up to Makeup? Umberto hasn't a moment to lose . . ."

Lara didn't exaggerate. The look they exchanged was one of pure hatred.

"You hets have slaughtered romance," Umberto sniped. His manicured fingers wove deftly through copper strands like an alchemist transmuting base ore into gold. I watched, fascinated, as he changed Joanne Carpenter into the elegantly dangerous Eloise Savage, the woman on "Riverday" who was romantically obsessed with Dr. Matt Jennett.

After signing in, Florence took me to her dressing room (a wasted trip yielding nothing significant), then upstairs past the greenroom to the makeup/hairdressing area presided over by Umberto, a prominent East Side coiffeur with his own salon on Madison Avenue. Florence told me to wait while she went back down to get Ames' permission for me to enter the taping area.

I asked Umberto a few questions, and the conversation led to the topic of "Riverday's" probable future.

"No style," he declared, affixing a roller in Joanne's auburn tresses. "Utterly disgusting."

She took her nose out of the script she was studying, looked up, and said in a hurt tone, "Thanks a whole heap."

"Lawdy, Miss Scarlett, I didn't mean you, honey!" His sinewy hands patted and pinched her cheeks affectionately. "Milady queen, you have reams of style, elegance, class, chic, oomph, pizzazz, not to mention chutzpah, moxie, éclat, panache, Zeitgeist, four-wheel drive, eight-cylinder brains and a chassis so snazzy that if you were only a Scorpio, I'd renounce the church and make an honest woman of you *stat!*"

Joanne groaned. "Would you believe, Gene, that's the best offer I've had all year?"

"Well, bitch," he huffed, "if that's the attitude you're going to take, return my engagement ring!" Pretending offense, Umberto put one more roller in her hair and blotted his hands on a paper towel. "All right, you heartless vixen, go roast your head."

"I'm done?"

"To a turn. Shall I autograph your bald spot?"

"Pardon me, you must have me confused with Ms. McKinley." Joanne rose from the chair with her head full of pink and blue rollers. "But what were you claiming has no style?"

"Life." He handed the actress her glasses. "If you'd paid attention to the grownups instead of trying to memorize that drivel, you would have heard me expound on life *sans* style as created by a medium controlled by hets with no romance in their souls. Their paucity of finer feelings is the manure for the dramatic weeds you now clutch to your sweetly underexplored bosom."

She stared at him coldly. "Ed wrote this script."

"I'm not attempting to rive away his laurels," he hastened to assure her. "*Ma petite ange*, Mr. Niven richly deserved the awards he won for silk-pursing sows' ears. He wrote marvelous dialogue, created situations that positively veered on the human. Not his fault the system dictated what he had to put in. Shall I proceed alphabetically? Abortion, adultery, baby worship, cheating, divorce . . . stop me before *R*, the network forbids romance."

"Signor Ciacionne," she argued, "romance is what daytime drama's all about."

"No, milady, precisely not." He sat her at a dryer. "Sex,

certainly. Adolescent passion, macho possessiveness, jealousy and revenge and domination, very yes. But pure love? Companionate affection? Quaint anachronisms they put in mothballs when they stopped filming in black and white."

"Behold who lectures me on the definition of love," she declared sardonically. "Umberto, you, of all people, shouldn't make sweeping generalizations about hets, as you call them."

"And why not?"

"Because, darling, you are yourself a sweeping generalization."

"Because you think I'm too obvious?" He positioned the dryer bowl over her head, paused before flicking the switch. "Milady, ask yourself the derivation of *gay* as coined a few decades ago. Or better yet, read the introduction to *The Gay Science*."

"Now it's a science?" she taunted. "*How* romantic!"

"A misleading title," he replied with condescending patience. "I merely mention it to stress the adjectival use in a defiant sense. Sometimes one *must* overstate to make society aware of its illnesses."

The actress yawned. "What's this got to do with the conversation you were having with Gene?"

"I was about to tell him I think Mr. Ames ought to take a chance and hire a gay head writer."

"That *would* be taking a chance."

"You needn't scoff. You'd be surprised what it'd do for the ratings."

"I suppose we'd pick up every sixth man." Joanne eyed the hairdresser. "You don't by any chance have someone particular in mind for the job?"

"Aahhh, that would be telling." He cut off the discussion by switching on the dryer, then asked whether I wanted to take a look at the roof.

"Yes."

"You can't go out there," he cautioned, "but there are windows to see from." He beckoned me through a portal at the far end of the room. I entered an L-shaped chamber whose vertical leg pointed back the way we came, enclosing the inner shell of the makeup room in half brackets. The horizontal leg of the "L" we stood in was a windowless nook equipped with table and chairs, a sink, refrigerator, cabinets and one tall unit of shelves stocked with snack food, utensils and various makeup supplies in tins, jars, cans, boxes, bottles, tubes and sticks. On the tabletop next to a tattered piece of Saturday's newspaper sat a moldy loaf of bread and an empty peanut butter jar with a sharp knife laid across the top, its blade still smeared with the sticky stuff.

"Pigs," Umberto sighed. "They never clean up, never make the beds. Look at that! One of them stole a whole big carton of collodion. You know how expensive that is?" Wrinkling his nose with distaste, he motioned me around the corner to the long leg of the "L," a narrow corridor with a cot along either side, one of them badly rumpled. Umberto inspected it, more and more disgusted. "Would you believe they even ripped off the pillow?" The sleeping nook had windows in its outer wall. They opened on a broad expanse of partly paved, partly tarry roof already tacky in the morning sunlight. A short flight of iron stairs led up to a sheet metal door that would have provided access to the roof except that its hasp was held shut by a shiny combination lock.

"That looks new," I said, pointing to the lock.

"It is. Security put it on yesterday."

"Why would anyone go out there in the first place?"

"To sunbathe in the buff," Umberto made a face. "Actors are like little children fleering at authority. Not that they'd set foot out there now, after what happened."

Just then, we heard a murmur of many voices growing swiftly louder. A tall, thickset man shambled into the alcove and shoved brusquely by us. As he passed, a sickening sour smell assailed my nostrils.

"Don't say you're sorry," Umberto piped in protest. The actor, paying no attention, flopped onto the unrumpled cot, rolled on his stomach and pulled the pillow over his head.

I recognized him. Ira Powell. He played Dr. Matt Jennett, the romantic male lead of "Riverday," the middle one of Florence's three supposed children on the show. Powell was one of the most popular sex symbols on afternoon television, but at that moment, I doubted whether any of his millions of adoring fans would have relished sharing his bed. I recalled watching Lara, on the monitor, go out of her way to avoid sitting next to him on the sofa. No wonder. Powell stank of sweat, alcohol and puke.

The cast meeting was done. A few of the actors stood in the greenroom engaged in low conversation. No one seemed very happy.

I felt weird, maybe even a little depressed to enter a room full of strangers whose faces and alleged histories I knew so well. So familiar did they seem, so much did I admire many of the people they pretended to be, it was hard to accept the fact that they had no notion—or interest—in who I was.

I had an absurd urge to clue in some of my favorites on the problems they didn't realize they soon were going to have to deal with. If only, for instance, Leo Jennett, father of the brood, knew that his new club manager was affiliated with the mob and wanted to use the family's supper club as a dope drop. Or if the eldest daughter Bella realized what was really in the letter that Eloise Savage etc. etc.

Lara waved to me. She was across the room talking with a short, stubby man I recalled from the days when Hilary handled PR for Trim-Tram Toys. In those days, Abel Harrison was an ineffectual executive floater, but now that he owned an ad agency and the casting office for "Riverday," he looked dramatically different. His once-straggly mustache had sprouted into a generous bush Oscar Homolka might have admired, and Harrison's dark glasses, bright clothes and hairpiece completed his transformation into something rich and strange.

His first question was inevitable. "What brings you here, Gene? Hilary send you?"

"No, I don't work for her any longer."

"What a shame! The two of you—"

"Are no longer affiliated," I said curtly. I glanced at Lara, but she didn't seem troubled by the incompleted remark. She, too, was changed. Umberto's handiwork, panchro base and the flush of rouge had effaced the woman I spent the sweet silent hours with. Now she was Roberta Jennett.

"Where's Florence?" I asked.

"On the set with Joe Ames. I don't think she's gotten your OK yet," Lara said. "I have a feeling she's preoccupied at the moment making thinly veiled threats."

"To whom? What do you mean?"

"Florence came in toward the end of the meeting," Lara explained, "but in plenty of time to catch the general gloom-and-doom mood. If Ames doesn't get a new head writer immediately, the show's in real trouble with the network."

"You know what this is all about?" Harrison said, pulling worriedly at his lip. "The sweeps are coming up, and the new rating figures are going to shift around a lot of advertising dollars. 'Riverday' has to get a facelift to convince WBS it can hold onto or improve its audience share."

Lara shrugged. "Ames has already axed a few of the older characters. Look what he was making Ed do with Ira's role! You think more heads have to roll?"

"*I* think so," the adman nodded gravely. "He needs a big gesture. 'A renewed commitment to youth' is the *dreck*-phrase they're using up at Corporate."

"*How* big a gesture?" Lara asked.

"Florence McKinley."

Like Alice stranded on the unwonderful side of an intransigent looking-glass, I was stuck in the limbo of a deserted greenroom until Florence got around to securing my clearance from the producer.

Lara couldn't stay long. She was in the second scene and didn't have time to answer any of my questions. On her way out with Harrison she promised to do what she could to speed up the process of getting me on the set.

Time passed. A voice on an intercom called for all the extras to report downstairs. That cleared the room. I wandered back to Makeup. Umberto was gone, but Joanne Carpenter still sat beneath the dryer studying her lines. As I entered, she glanced at her watch, closed her script and shut off the machine.

She gave me a wide-eyed smile that told me she'd exchanged her glasses for contact lenses. "Gene," she asked, "do you know how far they are in the taping?"

"They just announced the third scene."

"Good. Then there's still plenty of time before they're going to need me." She stood up and began to remove the thin rose-hued makeup gown she'd donned to protect the orange T-shirt she was wearing. "Want to go for a walk with me?"

"Where to? I'm still not allowed in the studio."

"I have to run out to Tenth Avenue to get a prescription refilled."

"Are you sure you've got enough time?"

"Hell, yes." She folded the gown and placed it across a chair. "They have to move the cameras and position them for the supper club, there's a whole bunch of extras to block and rehearse, they'll have a line runthrough, there'll be unexpected crises to solve and then a final dress rehearsal. It could take a good hour before they tape."

"All right. I'll be glad to come along, if you don't mind my asking questions."

"That's what I had in mind," she said, carefully patting her hair to make sure it was totally dry. Her head was still full of rollers. "Come on, Gene, I have to stop for a moment in Wardrobe."

I followed her into the hall and to the closest flight of stairs. "Doesn't anyone around here ever take the elevators?" I grumbled, my legs still stiff from climbing to the top floor with Florence.

"Only the kids. The older cast members don't trust the damn things, they're too slow and decrepit. Last year, I—" She caught herself. "One of the actors got stuck between floors and held up taping for hours. It cost Ames a fortune in overtime and ever since, he's had it in for . . . for that person."

"I suppose it's no use asking who it was."

She shook her head. "I don't want to be a gossip. The incident had nothing to do with Ed's death."

Wardrobe was two floors below Makeup. A big room with two tiers of motorized racks for hanging garments, it resembled a large dry cleaning store. No one else was there, but a sewing machine stuttered furiously in a small adjacent chamber.

Calling a greeting to the invisible tailor next door, Joanne rummaged through a rack of hangers. Each costume had a cardboard tag attached bearing the name of the character it was meant for scrawled upon it in red letters. I recognized many smart outfits I'd seen Joanne's character, Eloise Savage, wear on the show. But the one she removed was a simple white hospital gown.

"Fetching little number, isn't it?" she said, her lips screwed into a rueful moue as she rooted some more through her personal costuming till she found a plain blouse and skirt I hadn't seen her wear on the show for a long while. Draping them over her arm, she grimaced again at the skimpy bedgown. "God, I hope they let Eloise out of the hospital soon. Nobody looks any good in one of these damn things."

"Eloise is sick?" I blurted it out like an adolescent, immediately feeling foolish.

"T plus three. We're taping three weeks ahead of today's episode." Joanne laughed at my red face. "It's all right, I won't think any the less of you."

"Well, as long as I'm exposed as a fan, what happened to her?"

"Eloise is fine," the actress confided. "She's faking the symptoms of an obscure ailment so Matt will worry and fuss over her. Playing on his weakness for protecting vulnerable dames, you know?"

"Uh-huh." A familiar tendency. It was odd hearing her talk about her character in third person, especially now that Umberto turned her into Eloise Savage (all but the hair still in rollers, which Eloise never would have allowed any man to see). I was also amused—and dismayed —at the childish pleasure I felt in picking up a scrap of "Riverday" plot not yet revealed to the general viewership. The trouble was, I didn't know anyone I could tell it to, and what good is privileged information if you can't leak it?

Leaving the wardrobe depot, we descended one more flight and passed along another nondescript corridor that

would not have been out of place in Cocteau's drab im-
personal vision of the underworld.

Presently, we came to a door with a key protruding
from its lock. Joanne said it was her dressing room. I
reminded her of the security bulletin urging actors not to
do so with the key, but she shrugged it off.

"Haven't you noticed most of these doors have no numbers? It's hell when you're hurrying to make a change
and can't even find your own room."

"But aren't you afraid somebody'll steal your things?"

"If they want my clothes that bad, they're welcome to
them. That's all they'll get. I only carry a few dollars in
my jeans, and nothing but odds and ends in my purse. No
credit cards or checks. The only time I lock it is when I
change."

She opened the door and nodded for me to go in. I
stepped inside a tiny windowless chamber, carpeted and
neat but much smaller and plainer than Florence's dressing room. Joanne hadn't exaggerated; there really was
nothing of value. The makeup table held a box of tissues,
a cold cream jar and a paperback novel, nothing else. Her
battered brown purse sat on top of a bureau. The only
other furniture was a chair, a cot and a clothes tree.

She hung the garments she was carrying over the latter
piece of furniture, then, turning to me, asked if I would
mind closing the dressing room door. The redhead then
took hold of the bottom of her orange T-shirt and began
pulling it over her head. As she did, she turned her back
to me. I noticed no evidence on that smooth expanse of a
brassiere strap.

Other performers I've known are quite casual about
who sees them undraped, so long as it's onstage. The first
time I met Harry Whelan, for instance, he was rehearsing
Hamlet in the nude. But Joanne wasn't performing in

front of a camera at the moment, and she might just as easily have asked me to wait in the hall. The fact that she did not want the door open indicated she was at least a little concerned about her modesty, but why would she object to a passerby glimpsing her when the close-hand presence of a virtual stranger seemed of no consequence to her at all? Was it her alter ego, Eloise Savage, coming to the fore? Eloise *would* derive covert pleasure from a situation that was slightly naughty.

I pushed the portal shut and would have remained facing in that direction, but there was no point, the inside of the door was fitted with a full-view mirror. As I noted it, Eloise half-turned and our eyes met in the surface of the glass. Her T-shirt was halfway up. She looked at me and there was the briefest of hesitations before she pulled it up over her breasts, turning at the same instant so I saw her back again. Was I wrong or had there been the merest trace of a mischievous smile playing at the corners of her mouth?

"I don't like to go outside in old clothes once I'm Eloise," she said. "We sex symbols have to preserve our mystique. Oh, damn! I'm stuck. Can you help me?"

Her T-shirt was suddenly tangled in hair rollers. I stepped behind to assist. Joanne rested gently against me as I worked carefully to unfetter the garment without undoing Umberto's handiwork.

Spartan discipline has its limits. As she rested the length of her warm body against mine, I fumbled with the recalcitrant garment. She made no effort to prevent my eyes from wandering, and wander they did. Neither her baggy T-shirt, nor the TV cameras did her figure real justice. I forced myself to breathe slowly, but it was complicated by the fact that her chest rose and fell in unison with mine. It would be easy to succumb to the irrelevant attraction of the moment, and I didn't think she'd much

object, but my life had no need of further romantic com-
plications, so I made a great effort to concentrate and
succeeded to the extent of finally extricating the T-shirt
from her coiffure.

"There," I said, quickly retiring to a neutral corner,
"you're free now."

"Thank you," Joanne said, demurely holding her hands
in front of her bosom as she turned to bestow another
enigmatic smile on me. She then tossed the shirt over a
chair, turned her back on me again and proceeded to
strip off her jeans. Wearing nothing now but panty hose
and briefs, she selected a silk scarf from her bureau and
tied it about her head.

I made no more pretense of looking away. Except for
her surprisingly ample bosom, I saw she was slim almost
to the point of boyishness. Not an extra ounce anywhere.
She began to don the blouse and skirt she got from Wardrobe.

All the while I watched, I wondered who I was really
looking at.

"We're not supposed to wear our costumes outside,"
Joanne said, "so we won't use the front door." She opened
an emergency fire exit, ignoring the security bulletin attached to it. I stepped through onto the Fifty-third Street
sidewalk some distance west of the main entrance.

Turning, I saw Joanne close the door carefully so it
wouldn't latch. "No wonder the bulletins I read use so
many capital letters," I chided her. "You know you really
shouldn't do that."

"I know, Gene, I know, but everybody does. This
door's closer to the sound stage than the front entrance."

"And does everyone leave it unlatched?"

"I guess. If I go to lunch and slam it, chances are it'll
be open, anyway, when I get back."

"I see. Speaking of security infractions, did you ever go sunbathing on the roof?"

I never got an answer. Mentioning the roof reminded her that Niven landed somewhere on West Fifty-third. Joanne's wide hazel eyes turned upwards. Color fled from her cheeks.

"Gene . . . do you know exactly where he fell?"

I pointed west towards Twelfth Avenue, which was, fortunately, the opposite direction from the way we were headed.

"Good." She smiled wanly. "I just didn't want to . . . didn't want to walk past . . . you know?"

"Yes."

She was a good actress. She'd been pretending ever since I'd met her in the Colson-Ames office.

On the way to Tenth Avenue, we talked about Ed Niven. Joanne said she hadn't been close to him in so long that she had no idea whether he was or wasn't seeing another woman behind Florence's back, but she fervently hoped so. I asked her what she was doing Saturday when he fell, and she gave me the same answer Florence did: studying lines alone at home, no witnesses.

"An occupational hazard," she told me. "That's how anybody with a leading role on a soap spends most of her time."

I asked where she lived, and she named an address some twenty minutes' walk from WBS.

Turning south on Tenth, she took me to a small pharmacy a few doors in. The druggist on duty at the back of the store looked up and, as soon as he saw her, creased his face into an enormous smile.

"Oh! Oh! Joannele, you were *such* a bad girl Friday! You should look ashamed!"

Joanne laughingly introduced us. "Gene, meet my guardian angel, Manny Melnick. Manny, Gene."

The rotund young man shook my hand and bestowed a broad wink. "A *shayna maidele*, Gene. You're dating?"

"Manny," she interposed, "I've already got a mother."

"So? Till she comes to New York, I'm her surrogate."

"Manny, dear, this is a friend. Don't scare him off."

"Friends don't scare off, only *boy*friends." He peered at me over his spectacles. "You hear what she says, hah? What she means is a whole different story. So now have I scared you off, or are you really her friend?"

Before I could answer, she affectionately reproved him. "Maybe, Mister Melnick, you could spare five minutes away from matchmaking to fill a prescription?"

"You can always tell an actor," he declared, winking at me again. "Two minutes, and she starts to talk like whoever she's with." He took the empty medicine container from her, snapped his heels together and saluted. "Madam commands, Manny obeys."

He quickstepped his way to the drug department as Joanne began browsing through various cosmetics and personal care items. "He's got a crush on me, I think," she confided, picking up a tube of toothpaste and a bottle of shampoo. "If he were only single . . ."

"That's refreshing," I remarked. "You're one of the few beautiful women I've ever met not simply looking for a matching ornament."

"Listen, I've gone the pinup photo route, and got just what I deserved. Cardboard. At my age, a woman gets a little hysterical about never having a home and kids. I thought it was easy to give them up for a career, but now, I don't know. It could be very easy to lean on a man like Manny."

"You realize that statement could be construed as unfashionably unliberated?"

"Oh, hell, Gene! I was 'liberated' ten years before it turned into a cliché. Most actresses were way ahead of the carnival. I'm just about sick and tired of always hearing commitment equated with loss of identity." She regarded me pensively. "Sometimes I wonder if this so-called 'independence' isn't just a fancy contemporary term for being afraid to trust in anyone's enduring interest in what or who you try to become."

"Don't get mad at me, I was only testing to see how you'd react."

"Uh-huh. Wondering whether I'd hoist myself by the popular petard. Who were you comparing me to?"

That stung. I felt ashamed that I'd been measuring her in my mind against Hilary without giving a single thought to the woman I'd spent the night with.

Just then, the pharmacist returned with her refill. He put it on the counter and wrote up her order on a charge-a-plate. When Manny came to the shampoo, he stopped.

"Better not buy this brand."

"Why not? It's new. I want to give it a try."

He pointed silently to the label. She looked where he indicated and suddenly burst out laughing.

"Migod, Manny, just because it's got beer in it, I'm not going to drink it!"

"*Shah . . .*" He jerked his thumb at me.

"Manny, it's not something I'm ashamed to admit. I'm an alcoholic, Gene."

Which told me what she was having refilled.

Antabuse is used in rehabilitative therapy for alcoholism. The effect of disulfiram (the generic name for the drug) is to trigger off a severe bout of sickness in a drinker who goes off the wagon to any degree whatsoever. Antabuse is powerful enough to incapacitate a patient who sneaks a sip days or even weeks after ingesting the tablets. The drug is prescribed cautiously, since some people suffer worse attacks than others. In rare cases, mixing Antabuse with alcohol might even be fatal.

"Joannele," Manny said, clasping her hands in his, "one of my other customers on disulfiram developed a bad rash from an alcohol rubdown. You want maybe your scalp should turn red for the color cameras?"

"See how he takes care of me?" Joanne kissed his forehead.

"Did she leave lipstick?" he asked. When I told him there was indeed a smear, he beamed. "I'll never wash my face again!"

Blowing him another kiss, Joanne returned the shampoo to the shelf she got it from and chose another brand.

On the way back to the studio, I brought up the subject of the animosity between her and Florence McKinley.

"No mystery there," she said, stepping into the street to circle around a truck blocking off the sidewalk. "The Dragon Lady resents me because I was once close to Ed, and now that he's gone, you can bet she's going to use her influence with Joe Ames to have me written out."

"Did she really take Ed away from you?"

"She told you that?" Her eyes blazed briefly, but the fire quickly died. "I'm sure that's what she'd like to have everyone believe, but it's not true. It's my own fault the relationship ended."

"How? Why? It's obvious you've never stopped loving him."

"But not half so much as I adored myself in those dim, dark prehistoric times. Ed wanted the marriage *shtick*, kids and all. Smartass little Joanne thought her precious career came first. So I had an abortion without even telling Ed I was carrying his child. He found out, and that ended us. Eventually, he settled for the Dragon Queen, God knows why. I went out and bought a dog I could pretend is my kid, and here I am, stuck with one mutt and Numero Uno." A bitter smile. "Who says life ain't a soap opera?"

We crossed Eleventh in silence. The main entrance of WBS now was cluttered with five or six fans of both sexes armed with cameras and autograph books. The fat guy Lara and I posed for in the early A.M. was gone; I'd seen him trailing behind me and Joanne on the way over to Manny's pharmacy, but he wasn't around now, so I guessed he got all the autographs he'd come for. In the midst of the present knot of "Riverday" admirers I noticed an elderly bespectacled man in expensive, though slightly garish sportswear. As he shoved his way up the steps and into the front lobby, I asked Joanne whether she knew who he was.

"Yes. I almost didn't recognize him. His name's Woody. Why?"

Before I could reply, the fans converged. Joanne signed the proffered pages politely, pleasantly. One motherly woman in her sixties shyly asked if there was any chance "Martha" would be out?

"I don't know whether Ms. McKinley is involved in today's episode," Joanne lied, "but if you give me your name and address, I'll see to it that she sends you an autographed picture."

Effusive thanks. The woman jotted the information on a diary page and tore it out for Joanne to take with her.

On the way to the side door we'd come out of, Joanne grumped about Florence's aversion toward the fans.

"You're supposed to sign autographs, it's part of the

job. We're symbols, that's what keeps us working. We've got a responsibility to the viewers."

"But are you personally going to force Florence to mail that woman a picture?"

"Are you kidding? Forging the Dragon Lady's scrawl is Micki Lipscomb's job."

The barrier behind which lay the sound stage was painted with big white letters: *DO NOT OPEN DOOR WHEN RED LIGHT IS ON*. The light was off.

"I have to run upstairs and get the hospital *shmotah* I'm supposed to wear," Joanne said, "but I'll go in and check where they are first. If your clearance came through, I'll let you know."

"Thanks. I'll wait here."

She began to open the thick padded door, but stopped with her hand on the knob. "Gene, did I tell you everything you need to know?"

"Well, I may think of something else later."

"I hope you do." The smile she gave me was pure Eloise Savage.

She disappeared behind the door, and I was stuck once more on the unwonderful side of the looking-glass.

I waited a while, but nobody came out of the sound stage door. Lack of sleep was catching up with me, and I began to nod on my feet, but a sudden sharp voice at my elbow brought me awake.

"Well, well, how all occasions do inform . . ."

No mistaking that tart timbre. I turned and saw Hilary standing near me in the hall, hair tied behind in that tight knot which was generally a signal that she was in a no-nonsense mood. The lines of her light gray suit were as severe as her expression.

"Well, I imagine you're waiting for Lainie?" she asked.

"Maybe."

"My God," she muttered, "you sure work fast."

"Look," I told her, unwilling to involve myself in our customary verbal fisticuffs, "I'm going to pretend I don't know what you're talking about."

An angelic smile. "How traditional, Gene."

I counted silently before responding. "Hilary, the only reason I'm here is to investigate Ed Niven's death." It was not without calculation; it reminded her who had the license.

"I'm impressed. The Great Brain, Frank Butler, is so successful that he's opening a New York office, too!"

I told her my boss had nothing to do with my being at WBS. "I'm doing a friend a favor."

"A friend? Whom?"

Just then, the sound stage door opened. Lara emerged,

saw me and Hilary and froze. After an awkward silence more damning than speech, Hilary, acting as though she'd noticed nothing, addressed her cousin in a brisk tone.

"Jess Brass just called. She still wants to interview you. Should I tell her to go to hell?"

"No, she's too powerful to cross. Set it up."

"When and where? She says she'll come to the studio whenever—"

Lara shook her head. "No way. After the column she wrote this morning, she'd better stay far clear of Ames."

"Why?" I asked. "What did Brass write?"

"The truth. That Ed didn't hand in a new 'Bible' on time. That we're going to run out of storyline soon and Ames can't hire a new head writer fast enough. That our ratings will slip badly."

"You've got a spy on staff," Hilary observed.

"Afraid so. That's why Ames is livid. He wants to find out who the informer is."

"Well," said Hilary, "Florence McKinley is the only cast member well known to be in Brass' good graces."

Lara and I exchanged a look.

"All right," Hilary said, "I'll try to set up a lunch interview with her tomorrow. Okay?"

"Yes."

With a curt nod of her head, Hilary turned sharply and departed. I watched her till she rounded a corner and disappeared from view.

"She's in one sweet mood," I remarked.

"Her way of coping, Gene. Would you prefer histrionics?" Lara glanced at her watch. "I'd better get back on set. You're cleared, so come on. By the way, where *did* you disappear to?"

"Took a walk with Joanne Carpenter."

Lara shot me a sharp glance. "Oh?" A single chilly syllable.

"A prime suspect, remember?"

"Yes. Sorry." She promptly looked sheepish, for which I gave her points over Hilary. "It's not like me to play Jennie Jealous. But Joanne's a very horny lady."

"A very lonely one, anyway."

"Hey, junior, watch that empathic streak." She gave me a quick squeeze. "Hilary warned me about it."

It was my turn to say "Oh?" icily.

"Galahad in galoshes."

"What the hell's *that* supposed to mean?"

"That's what she dubbed you. My cousin says all a woman has to do is bat her eyes helplessly and you'll wade through a gutterful of crocodile tears to rescue her." Dimpling at my irritation, Lara gave me another affectionate squeeze. "Hey, don't look so steamed. *I* think it's a lovely trait in a man. In moderation."

"Meaning Joanne comes under the classification of immoderate?"

Kissing a fingertip, she touched it to my lips. "Lover, when it comes to storm warnings, you've got twenty-twenty."

Had it been Hilary, I would have argued, but that's because my former boss expects commitment without making any in return. Instead of objecting, I attempted to return her kiss in more traditional fashion, but Lara stepped back.

"Not now, you'll smear my makeup." Opening the thick muffling door to the taping facility, she invited me to go through. "Come on, Gene, it's about time I introduced you to the dream factory."

My first impression was confused: the vertigo of too much space, vast and cloaked in shadow. I expected the

"Riverday" sound stage to be big, but its immensity staggered me. When I stepped through the door, I found myself on a metal platform suspended in space. Looking down, I saw the concrete floor at least ten feet below. Far above me I could barely discern in the gloom a grid of cables, pipes and fixturing. I looked down again, then back up and estimated that from floor to ceiling it must be at least thirty feet.

Lara came up behind me and, placing her hands on my shoulders, whispered, "Some day, my boy, this will all be yours."

"My God, I had no idea it was this huge! How high is it, anyway?"

"Four stories."

A flight of black iron stairs led from the platform down to the studio floor. As we began to descend, I realized the reason it was so dim was because we'd entered on the studio's perimeter and most of the place was masked by enormous black burlap curtains hanging down from poles at the edge of the ceiling grid. Yards and yards wide, the coarse draperies blocked off most of the illumination from the arcs and floods suspended over the various sets, which, at the moment, were hidden from view.

Walking softly, we left the stairs and Lara led me along the edge of the place, a wall on our left—padded, with two more iron stairs leading up to the second floor of WBS—while on our right we skirted the cloak of the great curtains. We passed a makeup table equipped with lamp-ringed mirror and touchup supplies scattered and smeared on its powdery surface. A chubby technician in a matching messy smock smiled at Lara over his paper coffee container, but she shook her head, declining his services.

Further along, just before the barrier drapery ended, I saw a man hunched over an electronic prompting device.

A scroll of paper in it displayed what I assumed must be lines from the "Riverday" script just being taped. The dialogue was printed in enormously oversized letters; they were so big that only a few lines showed.

> Matt (on telephone)
> YES, ROSALIND?
> Nurse (on telephone)
> MS. SAVAGE INSISTS ON SEEING YOU.
> Matt (on telephone)
> DID SHE SAY WHAT SHE WANTS? SHE
> KNOWS I'M OFF DUTY.

That's all the lines that showed. But as I watched, the scrap of script began to crawl upward, vanishing into the prompter's upper compartment. New dialogue emerged from the bottom roller.

> KNOWS I'M OFF DUTY.
> Nurse (on telephone)
> SHE'S VERY UPSET. WE CAN'T DO A
> THING WITH HER.
> Matt (on telephone, SIGHS)
> WELL, I KNOW HOW DIFFICULT SHE
> CAN GET. BETTER TELL HER I'LL BE
> THERE AS SOON AS I CAN MANAGE IT.

I asked Lara what the man sitting by the prompter was doing, since there were no actors in the vicinity to be cued. She explained there was a duplicate roller on the set that moved in tandem with the remote. "He hears the lines over his headset and keeps the rollers paced with the actual flow of the scene. He's got a stop-start foot pedal that works both prompters, so we've always got the next line we have to say in front of our eyes if we need it."

"Ingenious. Why even bother learning the lines?"

"You're *kidding*," she replied. "How can you act, project emotion, move around if you don't know your lines? Prompters are only for emergencies, so if you draw a blank, you can pick up your line without stopping the tape."

Meanwhile, the big block letters crept up again. My mind boggled over the amount of labor the thing represented. I couldn't imagine how it was possible to turn five scripts a week into the huge scrolls required.

THERE AS SOON AS I CAN MANAGE IT.
Nurse (on telephone)
THAT'S A RELIEF. SHE WON'T EVEN
TAKE HER MEDICINE UNLESS *YOU*
GIVE IT TO HER. I SWEAR SHE
THINKS I'M TRYING TO POISON HER.
Matt (on telephone)
HAVE FAITH, THE CAVALRY'S COMING.
I SUPPOSE I'D BETTER HAVE A LITTLE

The crawler stopped in midsentence. The technician peeled off his headset, sat back and stretched.

"Problem on set?" Lara asked him. He nodded. "Come on, Gene, let's see what's going on."

We rounded the corner of the big black curtain and turned right into a long, wide vista of cable-strewn concrete. On either side of a central aisle, rooms and porches and business establishments stood in two long rows, like model environment booths at an industrial show in the New York Coliseum. I recognized them all, the various locations in which the action of "Riverday" unfolded, familiar places I'd seen at home on television. Near us on the left was the same Jennett living room set that Ames harangued the cast from earlier that morning. An actress who played a nurse was sitting on the sofa studying her lines; at a card table a pair of extras labored over the

Times crossword puzzle. All three performers were intent on their respective activities; none of them noticed us as we walked by.

To our right was the Jennett dining room, smaller and plainer than I ever would have imagined. Next to it was Eloise Savage's back lawn, the one with the swimming pool she liked to loll around in, showing off her legs to whichever man she was busy manipulating at the moment. Her lawn consisted of plastic grass mats unrolled next to one another, and the pool was a flimsy semicircular affair about a foot and a half deep. The water in it looked dirty.

We kept walking. I still couldn't see any cameras or working actors. Lara explained there was a second aisle parallel to the one we were on. "We have to go all the way to the end of this one, turn right, go through to the other half of the building and head back down the direction we came."

In addition to the sets themselves, the aisle had numerous wooden cabinets positioned every twenty or thirty feet: on their open shelves rested all sorts of tools, props and lighting instruments. Hammers and ratchets hung side by side with Fresnels and miscellaneous male and female plugs and connectors. Other shelves held books, towels, dishes, bottles, sealed jars with dark liquid that Lara said was flat cola, the beverage usually employed when coffee is allegedly poured on a daytime drama (a frequent occurrence).

"Doesn't that get stale sitting around like that?"

Lara stopped walking. "No. Props is very good about refilling drinkables. Why?"

"Idle curiosity of a fan. But look, I've been wanting to ask you a few more important questions."

"All right. Here's my office, step in."

By then, we'd crossed almost to the end of the long aisle. The last "Riverday" set on our right before the turn was Roberta Jennett's law office. Smaller than it seemed on television, it consisted of a single white pine and painted canvas wall on which was hung an undistinguished oil painting of a stallion. Against the wall was placed Roberta's desk and chair and a four-drawer filing cabinet.

Lara sat down in her usual place and I faced her, taking the client's chair across the desk. She was in her costume, a smartly tailored navy business suit, and her blond hair was pulled severely behind her ears. I was living a double fantasy: consulting the brusque, efficient Roberta Jennett, and also discussing a case with Ms. Hilary Quayle.

Remembering my night with Lara, I decided I preferred the real world to either fairy tale.

"First question?"

"Which cast members like to sunbathe nude?"

"*What?*" She laughed abruptly, more out of surprise than mirth. "Where'd you get that idea?"

I told her I'd been talking to Umberto.

"Naturally." Lara frowned. "Did he tell you what he pulled a couple of months ago?"

"No. What?"

"Me and Joanne and Kit Yerby had a long stretch before our next scenes. This was in June. We asked Umberto to keep the men out of the sleeping alcove while we tanned for a while. Actually, *I* wanted the privacy, the others didn't care who saw them."

"What happened?"

"We put our clothes on a towel by the door and lay on beach blankets. When we got up to go in, our clothes were gone and the door was locked. We had to yell our heads off for twenty minutes before Florence heard us and let us in. Our clothes were inside on the cots. Joanne was late for her entrance, and so was Kit."

"And you think Umberto was responsible?"

"He always denied it, but I think it'd be just the sort of thing he'd pull. He's a woman hater."

"Possibly." I tapped my forefinger on the desk top. "Possibly. But what about Florence?"

"What about her?"

"Maybe she locked you out, not Umberto."

"Florence? Why would she?"

"To get Joanne in trouble."

"Oh, I see," Lara said, bristling. "You have one talk with Joanne, and right away you're willing to believe her and not—"

"Just hold on," I cut in. "I'm not siding with anyone, I'm looking at things from all angles. And I don't even have a client."

"Gene, I'm truly sorry," Lara repented. "I'm just tense. Go on."

I got up, perched on the edge of her desk and took her hand. "Look, I know Florence is your friend, I'm not saying she was responsible for anything, but I have to eliminate the possibility entirely if I'm going to blame someone else. I'm asking about the sunbathing to see whether it provides a reason why Niven was on the roof in the first place."

"You think he'd make a special trip here on a Saturday just to sunbathe in the buff?"

"Lara, I don't have any answers or theories, just questions. If he was in the habit of sneaking onto the roof, say, with Florence—"

She stood up, taking her hand away from me. "Gene, I'd better check where they are."

"Ten seconds more. Tell me what the story is with Ira Powell."

Mention of the sottish actor made Lara look both sad and displeased. She came around the desk and peered into the aisle at a young man in Levi's carrying a ladder. "Gene, do you really need to hear? It's ugly."

"Yes."

"All right," she sighed, turning to me, "haven't you noticed a difference lately in Ira's on-screen character?"

"Matt?" I pondered it. "Not especially. He *has* done a few dumb things."

"That's exactly what I'm talking about. Matt's popularity as a character is based on him being the all-knowing kindly doctor *cum* father-figure. Safe, smart, sweet and sexy—that's the formula that made Matt a hero and Ira a star. And Ames is changing it."

"Why?"

"Why else? He doesn't like him. That's why he hired Harry Whelan. Ames is grooming him to replace Ira eventually."

"How? As Matt?" It was incredible.

"No. By cheapening Matt and making Harry's role, Todd, more appealing."

I got off the desk, shaking my head. "I'm surprised the network would allow Ames to tamper with the ratings. Matt's still plenty popular."

"Oh, it's a very slow, subtle change, it'll take months to cross-fade Matt and Todd."

"But Ira knows about it?"

"He's already seen a slight slack-off in fan mail. And instead of fighting back, he goes fey, holding his own wake. Drinking all night, heaving all over himself, stumbling in here without showering or even changing his shirt." She shuddered in pity and disgust. "I told you it's ugly, Gene."

"Can't he do anything about it?"

"I don't know. He ought to try while he's still got some clout left."

She took my arm and we began walking again. Leaving the office behind, we turned the corner at the far end of the sound stage. There were flats and other scenery piled all over. Bins full of lighting equipment, cable, props, rolls of half-used adhesive were jammed against the padded walls, and a matching set of black curtains hung down from the ceiling, making the area dim, eerily hushed.

I thought about Ames' despicable slow-motion destruction of Ira Powell. It occurred to me as we went through an archway and neared the second, parallel aisle that whatever the producer elected to do had to have been carried out, up to now, by none other than Ed Niven, head writer of "Riverday." I wondered which of the two Powell blamed more.

We entered the aisle. Its arrangement was identical to the first. On either side of the wide middle passage were sets, one next to another. The exit portal of a make-believe parlor doubled as the entrance to some fictional character's bedroom. The large and fully equipped kitchen of the Jennett supper club stood across the aisle from Eloise Savage's lofty library. I felt an irrelevant impulse to borrow the ladder I'd seen and browse among the high stacks for possible volumes on Hilary's want list (one of the extra little chores she used to throw at me when I was working for her).

Almost at the other end of the aisle I saw a group of people milling about in the midst of three bulky cameras and a pair of boom mikes. We headed towards them, and as we passed familiar sets, occasionally we noticed a cast member hunched over his or her script, oblivious to us.

"One other question," I said to Lara as we stepped along. "Did you ever hear of any cast member getting stuck in a building elevator and holding up shooting?"

"No. That one must be before my time. Oh, look, there's DB. You could ask him."

"DB" was the "tentpole" actor, Donald Bannister, portrayer of "Father" Leo Jennett. A tall, stoop-shouldered gentleman in his sixties, he had a pot belly, jowls and thick glasses, and at that moment, seemed pretty hale, possibly because of the deep suntan crinkling his benevolently wrinkled face. Bannister was a veteran of 1940s Hollywood, where he played countless gangster roles in films. I imagined the role of kindly restaurateur and daddy, Leo Jennett, might be a relaxing change of pace for him, especially since he rarely appeared more than once a week on "Riverday." As a matter of fact, I realized he hadn't been on at all lately.

Bannister was perched on a stool in another kitchen set tamping tobacco into a gnarled darkwood pipe. Lara introduced me to him by name and profession.

"Here about Eddie?" he asked.

"Yes."

"Dreadful," he mourned. "I only heard about it this morning. Been vacationing in Palm Beach, just got back last night. Dreadful." He drew on the pipe and tossed away the match. "Something you wanted to ask me?"

"Yes. Whether you know which one of the cast got stuck in an elevator a while back."

"That was Ira Powell. Why? What's that got to do with Eddie's death?"

"Maybe nothing."

I asked a few more things, but Bannister added nothing new to my scant store of facts. I was about to give Lara the nod that I was done when he pointed at me with the stem of his pipe and said, "I noticed you admiring the books in the library set, laddie. You a collector?"

"I used to work for one."

"Ah." He gestured toward the stacks of books I'd recently passed. "I donated all those. You can save your time looking, they're all worthless."

"So you're a collector, then?"

"I run a secondhand bookshop." He fished in his pocket and produced a business card, which he handed to me. His address was on Montague Street in "the Heights," a ten-minute walk from Florence's apartment. According to the card, the shop was only open three evenings a week.

"Strictly a hobby," he explained. "Drop in sometime, if you're in the neighborhood."

"Thanks. Maybe I will." I was half-inclined to ask him whether he might have one or two of Hilary's book wants, but Lara was getting fidgety, so I put the card in my pocket.

"DB," Lara asked, putting her arm through mine, an action which he noted with benign amusement, "what's holding things up? Shouldn't they be about finished with the supper club scene?"

"Well, they had to run and get a ladder and raise the chandelier," Bannister explained. "That new boy they got to play Todd hit his head against it when he came in, he's so tall."

"Poor Harry," I murmured, "what a pity."

Counting all the actors and crew members, there must have been nearly thirty people in the vicinity of the cameras. The technicians were moving around so much I couldn't get a fix on them all, but there were at least ten. The extras mostly were gathered on the sidelines in one self-protective clump. A beefy young man in the inevitable bluejeans stood on a ladder fiddling with the chandelier, calling directions to someone I couldn't see.

Practically underneath the fixture was my old rival, "poor Harry," as tall and slim and curly-haired as ever. Except for the man on the ladder, he was alone on the supper club set.

"That stocky fellow in the plaid shirt," Lara informed me, pointing to a fiftyish man near one of the cameras, "is Mack Joel, our assistant director."

"Where's the director?"

"In the control room. He watches all the shots on monitors and punches up what actually goes on the tape. Mack keeps *us* in line. Sometimes he's referred to as the floor director."

Just then, the technician on the ladder shouted to his invisible assistant and the chandelier rose several inches further in the air. Its new height was tested and marked, the man dismounted and removed the ladder, and the cast streamed back onto the set. Extras in evening wear sat at restaurant tables, actors dressed as waiters took up posts around the room. VeldaLee Royce, pregnant once more, stood by the cash register while "brother" Matt (Ira Powell) joined her and Harry exited.

Mack, the floor director, repositioned one of the waiters, then the booms moved closer and another crew member with a cigarette stub in his flabby lips extended a clapstick in front of one camera.

"All right," Mack said, "this is tape. Nine . . . eight . . . seven . . . six . . . five . . . quiet . . . four . . . three . . . two . . ." He gestured. The clapstick closed.

Animation. Like wax figures touched by a magic wand, the performers unfroze. Tinkling of glasses. Music. The Jennett supper club came to life as waiters took orders, poured wine, served food, bustled busily in and out of the place where the kitchen was supposed to be, carrying trays laden with cold, unappetizing food that the extras ate with seeming savor.

Watching the artificial scene with its boundaries and substitutes for truth, I felt a disproportionate disillusionment, even though I know magic looks lousy if you're standing behind the conjurer.

And now Dr. Matt Powell was called away from talking with his sister Bella Royce to take a phone call from his nurse, but I couldn't hear either of the Jennett siblings, Ira or VeldaLee, there was no Volume knob I could fiddle with. Then Todd Harry Whelan Jennett entered through a pine-and-canvas door flat and I could hear his lines perfectly.

The director stopped the scene and called Harry aside.

"What's wrong?" I asked Lara.

"One of the first things a theatre actor learns on a soap is not to project, it overloads the mikes. You have to say your lines in a natural voice."

"Isn't that a bad habit for an actor to get into?"

Lara nodded. "It eventually ruins the lazy ones. If you have any brains, you practice at home, you take classes, you do tours and summer stock just so your instrument won't get flabby. *Shh*, here they go again."

"Let's make this one work," the floor director said as the waiters collected plates, poured liquid back into bottles, backtracked like a film in reverse. "All right, nine . . . eight . . . seven . . . six . . . five . . . quiet . . . four . . . three . . . two . . ." His hand waved, the clapstick shut, the scene began again, but Mack Joel called an almost immediate halt while a makeup assistant ran to powder Bella/Velda's face.

"I thought the idea was not to stop the tape," I said.

"Within reason," Lara replied. "If she'd flubbed a line,

it might be left on if the mistake wasn't too obvious. But we romantic idols must *never* sweat."

I remarked on the absence of temperament during the proceedings, and she explained it was considered inefficient. "Temper is for nighttime television, Gene. It's harder to get rid of a series star on primetime. Even Florence generally reserves her snits for the greenroom or Ames' office."

"Speaking of the Dragon Lady, where is she?" Joanne's phrase slipped out. If Lara noticed, she didn't make an issue of it.

"Flo's back there, by the hospital set."

"But we walked right past. I didn't see her."

"She was lurking in the shadows. She and I have a short phone conversation coming at the end of the next scene. Flo likes to be totally isolated just before she performs."

"*Shh.*" One of the crew gestured to us, finger to lips.

"Places," the assistant director said. "Nine . . . eight . . . seven . . . six . . . five . . . quiet . . ."

The scene played this time without a hitch. As soon as it was over, VeldaLee emitted a victorious ululation, reached up under her skirt and yanked out a large contoured pillow, Bella's "child." She tossed it on the floor, jumped on it once with unmotherly contempt, then slung it under her arm, waved good day to everyone and exited with the extras. The cameras lumbered behind them on their way to the hospital set. As one rolled by, I noticed a copy of the shooting schedule taped to its side. It broke down the next scene into two parts.

IV-A	HOSPITAL/corridor	Matt, Nurse
IV-B	HOSPITAL/E's room	Matt, Eloise

We started in the direction of the general exodus, but hearing a voice behind me hail my name, I turned and saw Harry loping toward us, surprise all over his face.

"He-ey, Gene," he said, "what are *you* doing here? Back with Hilary? Last time I heard, you were stuck in Philly."

"Last time *I* heard, Harry, you were stuck at Hilary's."

Placing one hand on my shoulder, Harry addressed me with uncharacteristic earnestness. "Man, don't you know how crazy she is about you? Why in hell did you leave that stupid message on her machine? She—"

"Pardon me," Lara interrupted coolly. "You'll find me down the aisle, Gene."

As she strode off, Harry stared at her, puzzled.

"What's eating her?"

"Nothing that your sense of timing can't aggravate."

He squinted, trying to understand. Then it hit him. "You're *kidding!*"

"Why? You want Lara, too?"

"What the hell's wrong with you? Hilary never had any real interest in me. We're friends, that's all."

"I've got a different recollection of ancient history," I said. "Like a trip the two of you took to Washington."

"That was strictly business!"

"So you say. And speaking of business, how about these past six months you've been spending in *my* job?"

"Hey, look, you were no longer with her when Hilary offered it to me. After the two of you made up, she only let me stay on till I could find an acting job. Don't you know she wanted me out and you back in?"

"That's what she kept telling me, Harry. But once you left, she didn't rush to call me. She didn't call me at all."

He shrugged. "She was on the road last week with Lara, taking her to soap festivals."

"In all that time, she couldn't have telephoned?"

"What do you care?" he retorted. "You've got Lara now."

He turned his back on me and stalked off.

Scene IV-A.

Joanne was in bed in her private room at Riverday General, the same set I'd seen earlier on the Colson-Ames office monitor. Adjacent to the hospital corridor set, its door actually opened into that "hall," where Ira Powell, still bleary, ran through Matt's dialogue with a middle-aged character actress who played the nurse who telephoned Matt because Eloise Savage demanded his personal attention.

Lara stood in the aisle with me, her arm through mine, presumably for Joanne's benefit, though it didn't temper the smile I got from the redhead. Joanne's copper tresses had been combed out perfectly by Umberto, and she sat in bed looking lovelier than any hospital patient I'd ever seen anywhere but on a movie screen. She toyed idly with the premeasured plastic tumbler I'd seen Props place on her nightstand earlier.

"Okay, Matt," the floor director said, "continue on into her bedroom."

With a weary nod, Powell opened the connecting door. The nurse went off down the corridor. Only two of the cameras had been trained on them. The third was already aimed at the bed, but as Powell entered, it panned and backtracked to widen the shot and include him. As he and Joanne ran their lines (inaudibly, of course), another camera moved into position so the absentee director in the control room would have another angle to choose from. Lara and I took a few steps to the left to get out of the camera's way.

Sitting on the edge of the bed, the actor picked up the

cup and medicine bottle, leaning close to Joanne in the process. She shrank back against her pillows.

"Eloise," the director called, "you're supposed to put your arms around him, remember?"

"Mackie," Joanne protested, "*you* try it."

"What the hell's *that* supposed to mean?" Powell growled, shoving himself off the bed. "What are you trying to pull on me?"

Not waiting for an answer, the actor stamped over to Mack to complain. Joanne kicked off the covers, stuck her feet in slippers, grabbed a robe and hurried over to argue with the two men. The angry colloquy didn't last long. She returned to the bed, Powell sat back down on the edge and picked up the bottle and plastic medicine measurer again. They continued the scene from where they'd left off, but I noticed the director allowed Joanne to dispense with the hug.

Powell poured the "medicine," spilling a few drops as his hand shook, whether from malaise or anger or both I couldn't tell. He handed the cup to Joanne. She swallowed the liquid, made a face, spoke her next line, and waited.

And waited.

Because Powell was facing away from the electronic prompter, it was awkward for him to turn around and look at it. He solved the problem by getting up and pacing pensively with his back to the bed.

"Matt," Mack said with strained patience, "you can't do that during the take, she'll still have her arms around you."

"I *know*," Powell growled. "The bitch broke my concentration."

The director took a deep breath, but held his tongue. Never rattle an actor who's already coming unhinged.

The scene jerked fitfully to its conclusion, Powell forgetting one or two more lines before it did. The end was typical Eloise Savage: faking an attack of her pretended illness so Matt could fuss over her, calling in the nurse, cradling Eloise's thin body, comforting her as she smiled furtively over his shoulder for the benefit of the camera that dollied in for an extreme closeup before the image faded.

The director called a five-minute break while Powell skulked off set. He returned shortly afterwards in a new shirt, his face looking red and scrubbed.

"Okay, people, we're losing too much time," Mack complained. "How about skipping dress and going right to tape?"

"Yes," Joanne said, "please. I'm getting a headache."

The director pointed at Joanne and a makeup assistant hurried over and patted her forehead with a powder puff. Her face looked a bit flushed.

"Why not just make her wear a mask?" a venomous voice sneered behind me. Swiveling, I saw Florence McKinley dressed and made up to look like sweet Mother Jennett. But Martha never would stare such daggers at anyone.

"Places," said the director.

Scene IV-B.

Dr. Matt Jennett entered his patient's room and gently chided her. Eloise lay back on her pillow, cheeks reddening at the prospect of a quiet moment with the one man she *really* wanted. Matt sat down beside her, and his mere presence seemed to make her scant of breath. Opening the medicine bottle, he poured the proper amount into a new, clean measuring cup the size and shape of a whisky shot glass. Eloise used the opportunity of his proximity to put her arms around him and rest her head on his shoulder.

Matt put the bottle back on the nightstand and held out the plastic cup, but she wouldn't leave his shoulder.

The prompter froze in place. The dialogue didn't creep upward.

> Matt
>
> WILL YOU TAKE YOUR MEDICINE NOW FOR ME?
>
> Eloise
>
> OF COURSE. I TRUST *YOU*, MATT.

Her lips didn't move. Impatiently, Matt nudged her off his shoulder and tried to give her the dose, but she fell back against her pillow only to start up again, as if seized by a sudden cramp.

"She jumped the cue," Lara whispered in my ear. "There's a lot more script before Eloise fakes her attack."

Powell held the medicine in front of her lips, but she dashed it away with one hand and it spattered over the blankets. Her eyes were squeezed shut, as if in pain.

The cameras kept running, capturing it all for millions of avid "Riverday" fans who would have deeply envied my ringside vantage.

And now Ira Powell, improvising around the suddenly abridged dialogue, grasped the actress by the shoulders and shook her rather more roughly than it was in character for Dr. Matt Jennett to do.

Joanne uttered an extremely convincing moan.

Lara and I exchanged a worried glance. And I snapped.

Releasing myself from Lara, who still was holding my arm, I dashed onto the set, elbowed Powell aside and took Joanne in my arms, feeling the fever in her body even as the phrase, "Galahad in galoshes," popped into my mind. *Damn Hilary!*

"CUT!" Mack Joel howled at the top of his directorial lungs. "*THROW THAT STUPID LUNATIC OUT OF THE STUDIO!*"

Lara hurried to my side. Eyes wide, cheeks pale, she was clearly in a panic. "Polyclinic's only a few blocks away, Gene. Shall I call a limo?"

"First things first," I said, feeling Joanne shiver in my arms. "Yank the covers free so I can wrap her up warm."

"Wait, I saw a blanket—" She rushed off before I could stop her. I put my lips close to Joanne's ear and asked in a low voice whether the medicine tasted wrong to her.

"Yes," she whispered. Another spasm lanced through her. Joanne breathed rapidly for a time before she was able to continue. "Thought it was my imagination at first," she panted.

"Booze?"

"I think so." She shook her head jerkily. "No, I *know* so."

Quite a crowd was gathering around us. Mack took off his headphones and shoved his way through. Others mobbed behind him.

"Oh, Christ!" the director exclaimed. "She's really sick."

"Push those people back," I told him. "Give her some air!"

Authority figures are great to have around during emergencies. Mack immediately responded, barking commands at the gawkers to clear the aisle. Just then, I noticed Harry in the knot of onlookers. It surprised me how glad I was to see him.

"Harry, I need help."

He hurried over. At the same time, Lara returned with a thick tan quilt. I took it, wrapped Joanne up and asked Harry if he thought he could manage to carry her to her dressing room.

He nodded as he carefully picked her up. Joanne seemed so small in the arms of the tall actor, her head cradled against his shoulder, that she looked like a sick child being comforted by her daddy.

As he departed, I asked Lara where the nearest phone was.

"The business office," she said. "Come on. I'll take you the shortest way."

I followed her down the aisle. As we sped along, I wondered what had become of Florence. She was nowhere in the crowd.

Lara led me up an iron stairway similar to the one we'd entered by. As we emerged on the second floor of WBS, it suddenly struck me that I didn't know Manny Melnick's number. My intention had been to put Lara on one phone to call either a studio limo or an ambulance while I rang up Joanne's druggist friend for emergency advice, since I wasn't sure whether she should be moved or not. But I realized that I had no notion what his number was, let alone the name of his pharmacy.

Lara took me through a door marked FIRE STAIRS. I told her she'd better go on up to Joanne's dressing room and bring the purse on the bureau to me in the office.

She didn't waste time asking why. We climbed up a flight together, then parted company. Lara continued to ascend.

Hilary Quayle, hands on hips, was frowning at the studio monitor when I barged into the room. Micki Lipscomb stood near her, also looking puzzled.

"What's happening on the set, Gene?" Hilary asked. "Why are they all standing around?"

"Joanne Carpenter's been poisoned."

"Omigod!" the producer's assistant exclaimed. Micki's lips compressed, making her nose look even bigger. "Does Ames know?"

I didn't dignify the question with a reply, but instead told her to ring up 911 or WBS Security, whichever was faster, and arrange transportation for Joanne to Polyclinic, just in case. Squaring her oversized shoulders, she took a deep breath, but I didn't wait for a "Who-the-hell-are-you-to-give-*me*-orders?" speech. I closed Lipscomb's hand around the nearest phone and told her to dial. She hesitated one argumentative second, then turned her back on me and spun the dial three times. I figured she'd pick Security. An ambulance call might tip off the press. The police, for sure.

Hilary drew me aside. "What happened? Where's Lainie?"

"Upstairs trying to find the phone number of Joanne's pharmacist. I met him earlier." Briefly I outlined my suspicions. Hilary listened intently, absorbing every detail but offering no comment one way or the other. *Remarkable*, I thought. *Since when does Hilary soft-pedal a chance to play detective?*

Just then, Joseph T. Ames stormed into the business office, obviously trying to avoid a skinny youth in brown pullover, slacks and horn-rims trailing in his wake and waving a thin sheaf of papers at the older man.

"Franklin, leave me alone," the white-haired executive thundered. "I've got enough troubles without having you to deal with. Put that damn thing away, I'm not interested."

"Really? I'm sure they'd love to know that at Corporate." The kid reminded me of early Roddy McDowall.

His brown eyes, magnified by his spectacles, were cobra-cold; there was a supercilious slant to his mouth, and his voice matched the sneer.

Ames shook a finger in Tommy Franklin's face. "Threaten me, junior, and I'll boot your ass out of here *so fast—*"

"Come off it," the other interrupted, pointedly yawning. "I'm the only writer you've got left, you're not about to fire me." He shoved the batch of papers he was holding at the producer. "You saw Jess Brass' column this morning. You damn well better take time out of your precious schedule to read this. I—"

He didn't get a chance to finish. Ames snatched the papers away from him, growled that Franklin was probably Brass' spy, then clumped into his private office, banging the door behind him.

Franklin smirked smugly, waved the middle finger of one hand at Ames' sanctum and sat down at one of the desks to await the producer's verdict on the material he'd given him to read.

Micki hung up, looked at me and said, "They'll have a limo at the front entrance in five or ten minutes." Inclining her head in the direction of her boss' office, she asked, "Does he know yet?"

"About Joanne? I doubt it."

Rolling her eyes ceilingward, Micki slowly, hopelessly shook her head as she approached the producer's door.

"Hey," Franklin protested, "leave him alone, he's busy with something important."

"Oh, shut up, Tommy," she snapped. She rapped on the door of the ogre's lair. Ames roared an order to go away. I motioned Micki aside.

"Let me be the bearer of evil tidings."

"Be my guest," she said, stepping back. I turned the knob and entered the den of the beast.

The producer sat behind a huge walnut desk cluttered

with show business memorabilia, trinkets and awards. The five pages the young writer pushed at him were spread out side by side before him.

He glared up at me. "And just who the effing hell are *you?*"

"Never mind. Joanne Carpenter's sick."

He yelled for his assistant through the open door. Micki hurried through, stopping breathlessly beside me.

"Is Carpenter on the sauce again?" Ames asked darkly.

"I don't know any of the details," she replied.

"Well, what am I paying you for? Find out! Call Zack whatsis."

"That's what I was doing."

"What did Zack say?"

"I didn't reach *Mack*. I was trying to when—"

"Well, go do it," Ames cut in. "Why the effing hell are you wasting time in here?"

Biting her lip to keep from answering, she stamped out, bumping into Tommy Franklin on his way in.

"Who invited you?" Ames asked the writer. "Why don't both of you get out of my office?" Then he wagged a finger at me and demanded to know what I knew about Joanne.

"She says the prop medicine she drank made her sick."

"Actors!" Ames pronounced with great loathing, the corners of his mouth turning down as if he'd just sampled slop. "They blame everyone but themselves."

"Forget about her," Tommy declared. "Read my 'Bible.'"

Ignoring him, the producer asked if I knew how far they'd run the scene before they had to stop the tape. I told him. It seemed to put him in a slightly better mood. Again he bawled through the door at his assistant.

"What?" she yelled back.

"Have you got Zack on the line yet?"

"I'm just talking to *Mack!*"

"Punch him up on 4402, and give him to me." Ames grabbed his telephone and without preamble fired a rapid succession of brusque questions at the hapless floor director on the other end. I pitied Mack, ditto Micki, ditto anyone who had to work for J. T. Ames, with the possible exceptions of Florence and Tommy Franklin. (What had Lara called the young writer? *L'enfant terrible*—literally—of the midday mellers." Or did Hilary say that? No, she'd just referred to him as a "snotty twerp," hardly up to my old friend's usual level of eponymous invective.)

Franklin slung one leg over the edge of Ames' desk and perched there, playing impatiently with some of the producer's paraphernalia. He seemed especially enamored of an Emmy statuette. He hefted it in one hand as if it were an Indian club, possibly rehearsing for the day when he'd be able to wave his own in the air.

Just then, Hilary called my name. Going to the door, I saw her in the outer office with her cousin, who was holding Joanne's purse. I joined them, took it from Lara and rummaged through the bag till I found the plastic pill container of Antabuse. Its label had the pharmacy phone number typed on it.

"Manny? We just met. I'm Joanne Carpenter's friend."

"I remember. The 'just a friend' boyfriend. What can I do you out of?"

"Manny, brace yourself. I think Joanne's having an Antabuse attack."

"*Gevalt!*"

"What should I do for her?"

"First aid? Treat her for shock. Cover her. Loosen any restraints."

"I did both. What else?"

"Nothing. It's too complicated. Get her to a doctor."

"There's a car ready to run her to Polyclinic."

"Good. I'll call ahead so they'll be expecting her. Just don't panic."

"Then why do you sound so worried?"

"Gene, I won't kid you. How she does depends on her general physical condition. If she's basically healthy, she should weather it, but if she's got heart trouble or any of a whole batch of other complaints, it could be an enorous strain on her system. Just get her to the hospital *stat*."

As I hung up, Ames emerged from his office.

"Zack says we're okay," he told his assistant. "We can cut into the tape and save the scene." Ignoring four sets of angry stares, the producer shouted for Tommy Franklin.

The writer put down Ames' Emmy and sauntered into the outer room. "Well?" he asked in his usual insolent tone. "Are you going to read it or not?"

"I glanced," the white-haired producer said. "The second paragraph needs fixing."

"You're kidding! That's the one I thought you'd especially like!"

"I *do*. I just can't show it to—" Ames stopped himself and looked furtively in our direction. "Franklin, we'll talk later. Go see Zack on set, show him how to shoot around Carpenter. The bitch has the DTs again."

Hilary, Lara and I left then, which was lucky for Ames' neck, which I was about to break.

"Second paragraph of *what?*" Lara asked suspiciously as we hurried up the stairs.

"Franklin submitted a new 'Bible,'" I explained. "I've got a hunch there's something in it Ames doesn't want your friend Florence to see."

Neither Joanne nor Harry were in her dressing room. Donald Bannister, the elderly character actor, sat at the makeup table chewing on the stem of his unlit pipe.

"DB, where *is* she?" Lara nervously demanded. "I left her here with Harry!"

"Lass, calm down." Bannister gazed at us over his thick spectacles. "She got sick to her stomach again and he carried her to the rest room."

"Where is it?" I asked. "The limousine should be ready by now."

"It's around the corner," said Lara. "Come on." She darted from the room with me and Hilary close behind her. The old man followed. We turned right a few yards down the corridor and entered another hall perpendicular to the first. Not far off, Harry stood alone outside one of the doors.

"Harry," I yelled, hurrying up to him, "you shouldn't have left her by herself!"

"I didn't. She's inside with Florence."

Lara gasped. I uttered a terse oath and told her to get inside fast, but she was already on her way, Hilary right behind.

Harry winced, immediately grasping the situation. Six months with Hilary must have honed his intelligence. "Damn it, Gene, how was I supposed to know? I thought it was a good idea when Florence offered. It *is* a ladies' room."

"Not your fault," I told him, "but it's like putting a rabbit in the protective custody of a wolf."

Just then, Bannister—whose age had caused him to lag behind—joined us and motioned for me to step aside with him. I did.

"What's up?"

"Laddie," he said *sotto voce*, "is this likely to involve the police?"

"Maybe. Why?"

"I don't like to get anyone in trouble . . ." He paused meaningfully.

"Joanne might be in critical condition," I said. "If you know something, you'd better tell me."

"All right," he nodded grimly. "I saw somebody on the hospital set fooling around with the medicine bottle."

"*Who?*"

"Kit Yerby."

My head began to spin in forty directions at once, but before I could pin him down on details, the rest room door opened and Lara emerged, looking stunned. She held the door while Hilary supported Joanne, now wearing nothing over her panties and brassiere but the skimpy hospital bedgown she got from Wardrobe. She looked a lot worse: eyes squeezed shut, face flushed, body soaked with sweat, her breathing rapid. She held one hand pressed against her chest, the other on her stomach, and stumbled and tottered under Hilary's guiding arm. Behind her, last out of the rest room, came Florence McKinley, carrying the tan quilt. I took it from her and wrapped it around the sick girl.

Hilary told Harry to help Joanne downstairs. "By now," she said, "there ought to be a limo waiting for her at the front entrance." Bannister remained behind with McKinley, while I assisted Harry in carrying the actress down several flights of stairs while Hilary and Lara hurried on ahead and opened doors for us. Once we reached the ground level, Harry said he could manage Joanne the rest of the way. He led us through the halls of WBS, ignoring stares and questions from the curious. I followed him, with Hilary and Lara on either side of me.

Hilary murmured that she'd found Florence in the rest room taunting Joanne as she lay on the floor, cheek against the cold tiles. Lara said nothing. Glancing at her, I saw shock in her face that her friend Flo could behave so callously.

"Two minutes ago," I told Hilary, "I would've said McKinley was responsible for this, or at least considered it the most probable explanation."

"But now?"

I told her what Donald Bannister said about seeing Kit Yerby tampering with the medicine bottle.

"Kit was fired," Hilary reminded me. "She's working now at 'Ryan's Hope.'"

"Well," I argued, "maybe she sneaked into WBS through a side door."

"But didn't Kit play a nurse on this show?" Hilary asked. I said yes. "Then isn't it more probable, Gene, that someone borrowed her costume and Bannister mistook the impersonator for Kit?"

I nodded. Hilary was probably right. The elderly actor had been on vacation, hadn't even heard about Niven's death, so he very likely didn't know Kit was no longer in the cast. Maybe he just glimpsed a woman in white hospital uniform and assumed it was the actress he knew. I remembered the costume room Joanne took me to was virtually unattended, anyone could walk in and take any outfit.

It was looking worse for McKinley. She'd been lurking in the vicinity of the hospital set. I knew I ought to call

up Lou Betterman, but was reluctant to get Lara's friend
Flo in further difficulty till I was absolutely certain.

I glanced over at Hilary. Her attitude was puzzling me
nearly as much as the "Riverday" situation. Here she was,
in the middle of an investigation, a circumstance that
normally set her adrenaline pumping, but she seemed
cool and detached. I knew she'd surmised something was
going on between me and Lara, but in the past, purely
personal considerations wouldn't stop her from playing
detective. I just couldn't flatter myself that I'd grown to
mean *that* much to the lady.

Could I?

Lara couldn't leave the studio, she still had one more scene to do and, since the shooting schedule was being rearranged to work around Joanne, she had no idea when Mack might want to tape her and Florence, so she stayed behind with Hilary.

Harry was done for the day, though, so he came with me and Joanne as the limousine rounded the corner of Twelfth Avenue and skirted the western edge of Manhattan until it could turn into an eastbound street. We didn't have far to go, but the city's one-way traffic system made a straight-line route to Polyclinic impossible.

Joanne's breathing was a little less rapid at the moment, but she complained of a tightness in her chest and throbbing in her head and neck. As she leaned against Harry's shoulder, I gently pushed away a strand of hair from her eyes.

"Joanne," I asked, "have you ever had an Antabuse attack before?"

"No," she whispered.

"I talked to Manny."

"Who?"

"Your druggist friend Manny. He says you'll be fine," I exaggerated. "Basically, you're in good health, aren't you?"

She winced from a sudden pang. "What?"

"Your health. Generally good?"

She nodded weakly.

"No serious complaints?"

"S-such as?"

I was reluctant to specify, lest it cause additional stress, but we'd be in Emergency soon, and they'd want to know. "Look, Joanne, have you ever been diagnosed as having heart trouble?"

She looked at me oddly, but then another pain took her and she couldn't keep her mind on anything else. When she finally turned to me again, Joanne looked puzzled. Her pupils were dilated, and she squinted, probably unable to focus. She murmured something that was too thick to distinguish, though it might have been "Eddie." I repeated my question.

A furrow of concentration. "No, no heart trouble. Who—?"

"Who what?"

"Somebody else a—" The rest of the sentence was canceled by a cramp that doubled her up. I hated to keep pestering her with questions, but once she got to Polyclinic, I doubted anyone'd have a chance for hours.

"You were saying something about somebody else?"

"Y-yes. Somebody else asked me the same thing."

"About having heart trouble?"

"Mm-hmm."

"*Who?*"

But she was too groggy to bring it to mind.

Manny was already waiting for us at Polyclinic. With flowers for Joanne. She disappeared into another section of the Emergency ward, and the three of us—me, Manny and Harry—waited in tense silence in the visiting area. After what seemed like hours, a burly giant with bristling black beard and mustache stepped into the room and introduced himself as the resident on duty. He seemed slightly amused when three whey-faced young men converged on him.

"All of you relax," the physician told us, "we've got the reaction under control, Ms. Carpenter's going to be fine. Fortunately, she's got a good, strong physique."

Clutching his bouquet, Manny asked hopefully whether he could see her for a minute.

"Better make it this evening," the resident smiled, "she's already asleep. An attack like this usually exhausts the patient. You could leave the flowers with the nurse on duty."

I asked whether they'd have to monitor Joanne's condition, just in case.

"As a matter of course, certainly, but there's nothing to worry about. We'll keep her here overnight, and she should be able to go home tomorrow." Up to that moment, the physician exuded absolute confidence, but a sudden change came over his face and he seemed all at once unsure of himself. "There's just one thing—" he began, then hesitated, afraid to continue.

"What?" Manny anxiously asked.

"When she's feeling better . . . do you think she'd mind signing a few autographs?"

We parted at Ninth Avenue, Manny continuing west on Fiftieth, while Harry and I walked past the decaying storefronts and sun-flaked churches and *cantinas* lining Ninth. After I made a brief stop in a Woolworth's to pick up a few articles of clothing, a toothbrush and shaving things (in case I spent another night at Lara's), we entered a coffee shop a few blocks further north.

While we waited for our sandwiches, I told Harry about DB supposedly seeing Kit Yerby meddling with the medicine. "It probably wasn't her," I observed, "but she should be spoken with, anyway. Want to?"

"Want to what?"

"Talk to Kit for me?"

He gave me a sharp look. "Since when do *I* have *your* vote of confidence?"

I shrugged. "You've worked with Hilary long enough to pick up on some of her techniques. I assume you know her fairly well by now."

"Not half as well as you seem to think."

"Really? How about that time in Washington?"

"Oh, Christ, are you still brooding about that?" He sucked in enough air to declaim thirty lines of Shakespeare on one breath, but the arrival of the waitress with our food deflated him.

The Washington incident occurred during our investigation of a murder at Felt Forum. During a dress rehearsal of *Macbeth*, the actor playing Banquo was shot by the one portraying the infamous Third Murderer, an actor whose identity was being kept secret by the director—who, unfortunately, was the same man playing Banquo.

Our investigation took two directions. I chased down the facts related to the actual shooting, but Hilary turned scholar and solved the problem simultaneously by examining the three-hundred-and-fifty-year-old dispute over Shakespeare's mysterious Third Murderer. Her researches took her to The Folger Shakespeare Library in Washington. She never told me her intentions, though, and when I saw Harry making tracks for Amtrak, my eyebrows and suspicions rose, since he was a suspect. I tailed him all the way to D.C. and out of Union Station diagonally across the street to the Commodore Hotel.

The waitress left. Harry continued in a lower key.

"Truth time, Gene. I would have liked it to be more than a business trip, but the only reason Hilary asked me along was to speed the research at the Folger."

"Hard to believe," I said, biting into my BLT. "Especially since the two of you spent the night together at the Commodore."

He gaped at me. "Where'd you come up with that idiotic notion?"

I didn't tell him I listened at the door of his room. "I called her long distance, Harry, and she wasn't registered, but when I phoned *your* room, guess who answered?"

"Because we were busy discussing strategy for the next day, that's all."

"At eleven o'clock at night? Doesn't the library close around five or six?"

"Gene, we had dinner, we went to a show afterwards. As *friends*."

"Friends *and* roommates."

"No! Damn it, Gene, *I* was staying at the Commodore, but Hilary wasn't. A friend of hers at the Folger got her into the docent dormitory for the night. If you don't believe me, check it out for yourself!"

Feeling sheepish and more than a bit ashamed, I apologized to Harry.

"It's Hilary you ought to be telling this," he grumped, sipping his soda. "Mirabell and Millamant. Die before either one will be the first to say 'I love you' to the other . . ."

"Drop it, Harry. It's already done with. *Ausgespielt*."

"Why? Because Hilary didn't phone immediately when I quit?"

"Partly."

"Hasn't it occurred to you that the lady just needs some time alone? That she might be a bit scared?"

"Are we talking about the same woman?"

"Yes, smartass! The same Hilary whose daddy dumped her when she was a little girl. Is it any wonder she's afraid to trust—"

"Spare me the simplistics," I interrupted. "The time comes when you have to start making your own choices. Hilary's old enough and sure as hell smart enough to write her own scenario by now."

"Uh-huh. But what about Lara?"

I glared. "What about her?"

"What kind of script do you suppose is unreeling in *her* head?"

"You tell me."

"Wouldn't it come better from Lara? Or Hilary, since they seem to share secrets? Just ask them about Cousin Lainie's involvement with Abel Harrison."

"*Abel—*" I nearly choked on my food. "That's ridiculous!"

"Why? Because Abe's a comical geek and you're Prince Charming from Central Casting? You'd be surprised how much power that shrimp's got over who's hired and fired on 'Riverday.'"

"Harry, Lara didn't audition on a casting couch. Abel owed Hilary a favor."

"Undisputed. But not too long ago, Hilary found out there'd be a new male role opening up on the show. Whether you care to believe it or not, she wanted me out and you back. But she'd already called in her marker with Abe on her cousin's behalf. So she talked to Lara and asked her to pull some strings so I'd get a sympathetic reading for the role of Todd Jennett. Which Lara did. PDQ."

"That's it, Harry? Pretty inconclusive evidence."

"I agree." He drained his glass. "We might as well change the subject. What do you want me to do this afternoon?"

Damn Harry! I pushed away my plate, no longer in any mood to finish eating. I spent the next few minutes briefing him and trying to quiet my stomach.

"Manhattan South, Sergeant Francis."

"Inspector Betterman, please."

A lengthy pause. I identified myself for Fat Lou's secretary, waited a while longer, then was greeted by the police inspector's familiar flat, slightly nasal tones.

"Gene, good to hear from you. Still in Philly with that clown Butler?"

"Yes. Got a favor to ask. Will it cost, or can you bill me?"

"Depends. *Zug mir.*"

"Information. The WBS leaper."

"Classified."

"Might be able to help."

His friendly tone frosted over. "You back with Hilary?" Though he was her family friend since girlhood, he still resented the time she'd held back data so a murderer she pitied could slip out of town. I reassured him I was no longer with her.

"*Nu,* so come on over. You'll talk. I'll talk. Maybe."

"I'm not in town," I lied.

"You're not?"

"No. I'll have to send a messenger."

"Who?"

"Harry Whelan."

"Say, what are you trying to pull?" he groused. "You and Whelan, and you expect me to believe Hilary's not involved, too?"

"Honest to god, Lou, she isn't. Trust me."

"Sure, sure," he said with exaggerated courtesy. "Why not? You've always been straight with me, haven't you? Okay, send Whelan over. I won't promise anything, though, till I hear the questions, *fshtay?*"

"Copacetic."

"Now pay attention—your ass is in hock if you don't give me something back on this one."

"Lou, I'll do what I can."

"Do better, T.M. I expect. Period."

I had no idea what he meant by "T.M.," but he hung up before I could ask.

"Ryan's Hope," the soap Kit Yerby now worked on, tapes in an ABC studio within walking distance of WBS and less than a block away from the coffee shop where Harry and I stopped for lunch.

I escorted Harry to the door of the studio, prompting him on the way as he played back his instructions for questioning Kit Yerby and Fat Lou. The small building looked more like a warehouse than a temple of dreams. I told Harry when and where to get in touch, then left him and continued west till I reached Eleventh Avenue. I turned there and soon found myself back on the block where WBS was situated.

In the front lobby, the burly guard with the red face hailed me and asked how Joanne Carpenter was. I reassured him she'd be all right.

"Got something to ask you," I said. "Mind?"

"Naw," the guard replied. "Gaw 'head."

"You told me before that a guard got fired after what happened Saturday."

"Yeah. Woody."

"Old guy with goggly eyes?"

"Right." He nodded. "Wears thick glasses. He stopped by earlier."

"Why?"

"T' show off, I guess." An envious grin. "Brand-new sports coat 'n' stuff, y' know? Must've saved a lot of money over the years, now I guess he's gonna start spending on himself. Why not? He ain't got family."

"Why was Woody fired?"

"Those bastards upstairs wanted to shake up the rest of the staff, I guess." His indrawn breath hissed between clenched teeth. "He was on duty when Niven creamed himself on the sidewalk. Woody's mistake was to tell a Channel 14 newsman that Niven must've sneaked into the building. He might as well've yelled, 'C'mon on over and rip us off!' So they shitcanned Woody the next morning with only a year to retirement."

I well remembered the late telecast that shook me out of my goldfish-gawking reverie, and I also recalled feeling sorry for the elderly security guard on it whose big mouth probably bought himself a pink slip. That was Woody, and I saw him twice since that evening, though I didn't quite recognize him the first time. His face didn't register in its proper context till, noticing him walking up the front steps of WBS, I asked Joanne if she knew his name.

Woody was the shabby derelict I'd seen sitting on a park bench Monday evening on the Brooklyn Heights promenade, his back to the river, his owlish eyes gaping up at the great lighted picture window at the back of Florence McKinley's apartment.

There was less chaos on the sound stage than I'd expected. The cameras were taping and Tommy Franklin sat at a writing table on one of the vacant sets scribbling furiously on a lined paper tablet while a production assistant stood by to snatch the finished sheets of dialogue as soon as Franklin was done with them.

Florence and Lara saw me first and hurried over. I said Joanne Carpenter would survive. Lara was relieved, of course, and Florence did her best to conceal her disappointment.

"Will you be home this evening?" I asked the older actress.

"Certainly." She frowned. "Why?"

"I may stop by to report." I paused while she chewed on it before I added the codicil. "If I do, I'll have a friend with me."

"Who? I don't permit strangers in my home."

"This is one time you're going to have to break the rule."

I hadn't expected her to accept it easily. We wrangled, but I wouldn't budge or explain, so Florence, consumed with curiosity, or perhaps anxiety, consented on the condition that Lara be there as a witness.

Lara nodded, but a sudden thought made her frown. "Can you not make it too early, Gene? I've got a—" She stopped abruptly.

"What?"

"A business appointment," Lara mumbled, avoiding my eyes. Florence suddenly declared that she felt chilly. Lara seized the opportunity to volunteer to fetch her friend a sweater.

It was a ruse, of course. When Lara was gone, Florence drew me aside. We stepped onto a dusty, seldom-used patio set, where the actress began to pester me for details.

I hedged. "I don't have all the facts yet. By tonight, I may."

"Good," she said smugly. "The sooner you expose that bitch, the better."

"Who? Joanne?"

"Who *else*?" she shrilled, momentarily forgetting where she was. Someone shushed her, and she dropped her voice to a whisper. "Joanne murdered my Eddie, then tried to blame it on me by putting his clothes in my dressing room. When that didn't work, she poisoned herself today so *that'd* look like *my* fault, too!"

It took an effort of will not to walk away from her, but I didn't have to endure Florence for long. Discovering that I was in the studio, Mack Joel, the floor director, hurried over to find out Joanne's condition. When I told him, he seemed genuinely relieved.

"She's the sweetest gal in the whole cast," the stocky director asserted. "Do me a favor, will you? Take the news up to Micki Lipscomb in the 'Riverday' office? She'll have to work out the revised taping run for the next few days."

"Sure," I agreed, glad of a reason to get away from Florence McKinley.

The business office was empty. I walked in and was about to call to see if anyone was there when the door to

Ames' private sanctum opened. Micki Lipscomb came out.

She was in an extreme state of agitation that seemed worse in contrast to her usual unflappability. Her face was pasty white.

"What's wrong, Micki?"

She opened her mouth to answer me, but her lips got no further than a ghastly parody of a grin. Her legs gave out and she began to slump to the floor. I ran and caught her. Easing the tiny woman down, I checked her mouth, loosened restraining clothing, monitored her pulse. She was unconscious, but otherwise seemed okay.

Stepping around her, I peeked into Ames' office. It was a mess. The desk top was swept clean. Trophies, papers and memorabilia were scattered over the floor. Prone on the carpet, one cheek pressed against it, lay Joseph Ames. Blood trickling from a wound behind his left ear stained the rug. A few inches away, its edge smeared red, I saw the Emmy statuette Tommy Franklin had been hefting in the air earlier that afternoon.

I felt for, found an irregular pulse. As I turned, Micki stirred. I got her to a chair, made sure she wouldn't go into another faint, then handed her the phone and suggested this time she make it an ambulance.

Nevertheless, she dialed Security. She croaked a few sentences into the instrument, then hung up and looked earnestly into my eyes.

"Gene," Micki said, still hoarse, "*I* didn't do it!"

Four hours later, I sat in the cool semigloom of Lara's unlighted penthouse, sipping scotch and feeling sorry for myself. Which isn't easy when you're sampling $75-a-bottle Ballantine's for the first time in your life.

I managed to catch Lara before she left the studio. She turned down my dinner invitation, explaining that she had an unbreakable business appointment with Abel Harrison, but promised to meet me sometime after nine at Florence's. "Here," she said, handing me the keys to her apartment, "you can freshen up at my place, love. Help yourself to whatever food you find." She kissed me goodbye and I hailed a taxi, telling myself not to believe Harry, that if he hadn't opened his big mouth, I wouldn't have given Lara's "business appointment" a second thought.

The doorman accompanied me upstairs to make sure the keys fit, but he recognized me from the morning, anyway. Inside, I opened the parcel of necessaries I'd purchased on Ninth Avenue and went to the bathroom to shower, shave and change clothes.

The styptic Lara loaned me that morning ought to have tipped me off. Women don't use it that much, I'm told. When I opened her medicine chest, I discovered one whole shelf loaded with men's toiletry articles.

And what the hell did you expect, Lancelot and Elaine? I chided myself. *You've been in Lara's life a grand total of two point five days.*

True, but why did it have to be that twerp Abel Harrison? A clown, a total nebbish, and come to think of it, wasn't he married?

But Abel handled the casting for "Riverday" and had valuable West Coast contacts, too.

The doorbell rang. I glanced at my watch, squinting in the dimness to see the numbers. Harry was right on time with his report. I flicked on the hall light, put my eye to the peephole—and felt a sudden surge of joy well up within.

She broke the date!

I swung the door wide, stepped onto the threshold and, despite the fact that Lara was carrying a large brown paper bag, threw my arms around her, package and all. Our lips met.

I froze in midkiss.

Taking a backward step, Hilary said matter-of-factly, "You obviously mistook me for Lainie." Saying nothing, I waited for the inevitable barbed comment, but it didn't come. She merely apologized for not phoning on ahead, then asked if she could enter with a politeness that held no trace of sarcasm. A bit numb, I stepped aside and she walked in.

She no longer wore a business suit, but instead had on a summery green halter top with slacks of a deeper shade of the same color. Uncustomarily casual for her, but flattering.

She took the paper bag to the dining area, put it on the table and began to remove several white cardboard cartons from it. "Hope you don't think it's presumptuous," she said, "but Harry said you'd be waiting here for him around six, and I'm only too familiar with the usual state of Lainie's larder. So I took the liberty of picking up dinner from Uncle Wong's."

"But where's Harry?"

"Oh, he couldn't make it. I promised him I'd relay the information you asked him to root out. Okay?"

It wasn't really, but I had to admit there was nothing decent in Lara's refrigerator, and I was hungry. I was also curious to see how long Hilary could keep up the sweetness-and-light bit.

"Okay," I nodded. "Let's eat."

She knew Lara's kitchen better than I, so Hilary got bowls and spoons and ladled out Winter Melon Soup, my favorite. She sat down and began to talk as we ate.

"Harry says Kit Yerby was taping all morning at 'Ryan's Hope' and has witnesses to prove it. On Saturday, when Niven died, she was at a soap opera festival, just like me and Lara, so you can totally write off Kit."

"Okay," I said, sipping soup, "now how'd Harry do with Lou Betterman?"

"Remarkably well." She patted her lips with a napkin, then ticked off points on her fingers. "First, the reason they know Niven fell from the roof, not out of a window, is that they found tar on his feet and matching gouges on the roof. Second, Florence, Joanne Carpenter and Ira Powell have no verifiable alibis."

"Hm."

"I think, just the same, Gene, I'd count out Powell. I can't picture him in drag fixing Joanne's medicine." A suggestion spoken without the least condescension. She was beginning to make me nervous. I wasn't used to Hilary this way.

"Okay," I prompted, "go on. Anything else?"

"Yes. Saturday, Tommy Franklin was home working on the 'Riverday' 'Bible' he gave to Ames in synopsized form this afternoon. He's been updating it constantly for months."

"Is his alibi tight?"

"Seems to be. While he was working, there was a friend in the other room watching TV. Umberto, the show's hair stylist. You've met him?"

"Sure have. Is that the lot?"

"No." She held up a hand to put the conversation on standby while she opened a container of spring rolls. After they were distributed and condiments put on the table, Hilary produced two bottles of Kirin, removed their caps and poured, adjusting the beads to the heights we each preferred. She was taking too long, so I knew her next item was important. Another time, I might've nagged her to get to it, but if she chose not to be her usual smug, didactic self, out of respect for the effort at self-control, the least I could do was keep my mouth in neutral.

After a long swallow of beer, Hilary said, "Lou found Niven's clothes at the studio over the weekend. A bloody shirt, slacks, socks, a pair of shoes. The forensic team's picking the stuff to pieces."

"Where'd his men uncover the things?"

"In Joanne Carpenter's dressing room."

I put down my chopsticks. I was upset. So that was where Flo hid Niven's clothing.

I said, "Then I imagine Joanne is now Lou's prime suspect."

Hilary nodded. "He told Harry he was having her tailed. Lou was curious where you and Harry and she rode off to when she was wearing nothing but briefs and a hospital gown."

Uh-oh. Trouble. I'd told Lou I wasn't in New York, and he already knew I was lying. But how? A plainclothesman watching Joanne wouldn't necessarily have recognized me. Then I remembered the young "fan" with the camera slung around his neck who'd been waiting in front of WBS at an astonishingly early hour. He took a photo of me and Lara, and I signed "Tom Mason" in his autograph book. That's what Fat Lou must've meant when he called me "T.M." on the phone.

"What's the matter?" Hilary asked. "You look worried."

"I am. I just realized I could lose my license."

She didn't comment, just served the Scallops and Straw Mushrooms—bland, delicious and light enough to keep us from feeling bloated all evening. Pushing away the empty carton, she rested a hand on mine for a moment.

"Gene, what can I do to help?"

"Short of solving this mess, nothing much. I lied to Lou, and now I have to come up with something for him, or else. Trouble is, the only things I can hand him are exactly what I'm trying to find alternatives for, but can't."

She looked as if she might say something, but changed her mind. Lowering her eyes, she paid attention to her dinner. I ate some, drank beer, thought things over yet again. I wanted to lay out what I'd uncovered for Hilary, see what her opinion was, but I was afraid she'd concur on the obvious. Also, I wasn't positive whether I really wanted Hilary's help, or just sought an excuse to close the gap between the two of us, and if that was the case, forget it, it wasn't fair to Lara. On the other hand, my inclination to bring her into it might be nothing more than force of habit.

I chewed on the problem along with my dinner, decided at length that there was no harm, at least, in telling her about the most recent development. She'd get wind of it at WBS, anyway.

"Do you know what happened to Ames after I saw you?"

"No."

I told her.

"There does seem to be an epidemic of violence around WBS," Hilary remarked. "How badly is he hurt?"

"He'll pull through."

"Figures. Producers have thick skulls."

A touch of vintage Hilary. I knew she couldn't keep up the act forever. I told her I was with Ames up to the time he was put in the limo for Polyclinic. "He came around for a few minutes. Says he walked into his office, bent down to tie his shoe when someone crouching behind his desk tipped it over on him. Before he could get free, he was knocked behind the ear with his Emmy."

"I'd call it poetic justice," she said, "except that dramatic justice seems more appropriate."

Hilary was sounding more and more like her old self. *Good.* When she turned on me, I was all ready to bring up "Galahad in galoshes."

"Did you find Ames, Gene?"

"No, Micki Lipscomb did. I arrived right afterwards and caught her when she collapsed." The latter detail frankly was to set her up; I was sure Hilary couldn't resist such a gambit. But she didn't utter a syllable. (I wondered whether she realized how effectively she was getting on my nerves by not getting on my nerves.) "Anyway," I added, "Ames is recuperating now at Polyclinic."

"Any theories, Gene?"

"Why he was attacked? Yes. Remember the proposed 'Bible' Tommy Franklin handed him earlier? Last I saw of it, Ames had it spread out on his desk, but after they took him to the hospital, I made Micki root through his things, and guess what?"

"No 'Bible.'"

"Correct."

"Well," Hilary shrugged, "that in itself doesn't prove much, though—"

Lara's intercom interrupted her. I went to the button, pressed and told the doorman to send up the man in the lobby. Hilary raised an eyebrow, but I'd allowed her to play her own pregnant pause, so now it was her turn to wait.

A moment later, the doorbell rang. I opened it. In came Willie Frost, Hilary's personal attorney. A short, slightly paunchy man in his forties, Willie had on his usual three-piece ensemble, despite the warm weather. His brown hair, once crew cut, now was stylishly long, and he'd given up his old clean-shaven appearance for a mustache, close-trimmed beard and side whiskers.

"Gene, Hilary, good to see you both again."

"It's been a while," I said. "Still making it hot for Ma Bell?" Willie had a personal vendetta against the telephone company, and did lots of little things to drive its people crazy.

"I'm taking it easy on them lately," he replied, smiling like a slightly bored Olympian. "It's *such* an unfair fight." His lofty tone left no doubt whose side held the short odds.

"Willie, hello," said Hilary, rising to shake his hand. "What brings you here?"

"*I* did," I told her, deliberately dangling insult bait.

Her mouth opened, but shut again. A two-beat pause before she trusted herself to ask me, a bit too sweetly, whether I'd care to enlighten her. I could practically taste the sardonic "brightness" she swallowed unspoken.

"Willie's a kind of favor to Lara," I stated. "I've got to take him to Brooklyn Heights now. Care to come along?"

Hilary nodded her head grimly.

We took my car. I drove slowly, since we were early. On the way, I gave Willie the details. Hilary occasionally asked me a question, but mostly she remained silent.

It was too early to visit Florence. Lara wouldn't arrive till after nine, and her presence was a precondition, so we parked on a side street near Montague and walked to the business thoroughfare of "the Heights." The three of us spent about thirty minutes in a bistro with brandy and coffee. Willie entertained us with tales of his early exploits as an insurance attorney, and Hilary told about the time she investigated an alleged case of arson in the Christmas decorations industry, an exploit that took place before I'd begun working for her.

After we'd been gabbing for a while, I remembered that Donald Bannister's bookshop was on Montague Street. I got out the card he gave me and checked. He was open that evening. I mentioned it and Hilary immediately was interested, which came as no surprise. No matter what else she might be doing, Ms. Quayle never can resist a secondhand bookstore.

The Night Owl was two blocks away, a street-level establishment with an overhead sign of a bespectacled owl poring over a book with the title, "I Don't Give a Hoot!" There was an outside table loaded with miscellaneous volumes, all priced at 50¢ each. The inside of the shop was narrow, dimly lit and crammed with warped, canted bookshelves, some fashioned from orange crates. Books of varying sizes and thicknesses, hardbound, paperback, were assorted by subject, but otherwise followed no consistent arrangement. The optimum browsing mode, according to Hilary. The back wall, partly visible down the uneven aisles, was entirely devoted to the lively arts. This was also good form, so far as Hilary thought. A good used book dealer always has a specialty.

At the moment, there were no customers. Donald Bannister sat alone at the front of the store, eyes half-closed, pipe in mouth. The frantic day at the studio took its toll. His jowls seemed deeper, his forehead more severely creased with worry lines. But when he saw us, his face grew more animated. He waved at us to come in.

"Laddie," the elder statesman of "Riverday" hailed me, "I didn't suppose you'd come this soon! Welcome! Help yourself to some mulled wine."

Bannister shook hands with Willie, whom I introduced, and also greeted Hilary. They were already acquainted with each other from times she'd spent at WBS conferring with her client and cousin. He gestured for us to gather round the check-out table. Next to the cash register on top of a hot plate was a metal pot with a ladle in it steeped in a scarlet liquid redolent of cinnamon, cloves and apples. Willie declined a drink and wandered off to examine the nonfiction, but Hilary and I accepted the paper cups the actor filled for us.

"Very nice," Hilary said, "but isn't it a bit early in the season? I usually associate hot wine punch with autumn."

"True, true," Bannister laughed, "but at my age, lass, it sometimes pays to rush things." He sat down again behind the counter and, running a hand through his gray hair, regarded me with a rueful smile. "Quite a day you picked to get a behind-the-scenes glimpse, eh? The plot in the Jennett kitchen was thickening, but in the hospital, it was sickening." He intoned the latter melodramatically.

"Well, taking all that into account, I was generally impressed with the way 'Riverday' is put together," I said, sipping at the wine before adding, "and also disappointed."

"Naturally. Gods don't look good up close. Unquote." He gestured with his pipe stem like a professor stressing some obscure point. "Soap opera fantasy is meant for the living room. It's practically impossible for the fans to understand that, but even some of the kids we get on the show have a hard time with it."

"In what way?" Hilary asked. "You mean the younger actors?"

He nodded. "They haven't yet learned how to distance themselves from their roles. See, there's hardly enough time to get the lines down, let alone polish. The plot is unpredictable, anyway, so the tendency is to mine your own emotional memories . . . and that can draw blood."

"How?"

"A common example, lass, is when a new cast member has to pretend to be in love with some actress he's just met, and maybe doesn't even like. There's never time on a soap for intensive rehearsing, so he'll probably just invest her with an 'as-if' affection he really feels for his wife or girl friend or lover. He plays love scenes with the actress. It goes on for weeks or maybe even months, and then the head writer decides to bring in a new man to steal away his ersatz love. Bang! All of a sudden, he actually feels threatened, sexually inadequate."

"What happens then?" I asked.

"If he's lucky enough to be paired with a mature actress, she'll see the symptoms and spend a little time with him between scenes. Nothing significant, understand, just a few human fellow-actor chats to remind him that, after all, the show is only make-believe."

Hilary refilled her cup. "Lara's told me she often has to sit with Florence to 'talk her down' from some attack of Jennett family anxiety."

"Well, that's understandable," said Bannister, "though you'd think Ms. McKinley is old enough to know better. But the role of Martha is her hiding place, don't y' see? She's *become* the mother she never had herself. Don't know what she'd do if they ever tried to kill off Martha."

Hilary and I exchanged glances, but said nothing.

The conversation passed on to the topic of "Riverday's" fans. The actor pinched the bridge of his nose with index finger and thumb, closing his eyes. He looked worn out. "The letters we get," he soliloquized. "They send presents and propositions to the heroes and poisoned candy to the villains. Two or three months ago, a woman wrote inviting me to spend a weekend with her. Among other things, I was supposed to escort her to *her husband's* annual company dinner. She said he'd given her full permission to do whatever she and I wished. She confided that she goes to bed every night with my picture under her pillow."

"Did you accommodate her?" Hilary asked drily.

"Oh, I said no with great difficulty," he replied in an ironic tone. "It was quite a test, too. As an added inducement, she included a photo of herself. Three hundred pounds, I do *not* exaggerate, and dressed in a strapless evening gown."

Hilary and I chuckled, but it was hollow laughter. I wondered how many years of suffering that man and woman endured before reaching their unusual agreement. A grotesque example, perhaps, but not all that different from millions of Americans with no one to rejoice or cry with except strangers performing improbable morality dramas five days a week, same time, same channel.

"It's an inescapable paradox," Donald Bannister asserted, knocking the dottle from his pipe into an ashtray. "You see flesh-and-blood people moving and speaking on TV and you can't help but think the puppets are the characters you fall in love with. It's like that Fred Brown science-fiction story where a man conceives a passion for a woman telepathically conjured up by an intelligent cockroach. It's not so different with soap actors. I mean, you might just as well try to share the soul of a Chopin étude by going to bed with the piano tuner."

The door opened and a customer entered, seeking information from Bannister. The actor excused himself, and Hilary used the opportunity to begin browsing through the shop. I did the same, choosing another aisle. I saw Willie. He pointed to his watch.

"Ten more minutes tops, Gene."

"Fine. I leave you the task of prying Hilary loose."

The attorney smirked. "How many favors do you think I owe?"

I walked to the back of the store, my eyes automatically running swiftly along the spines of faded bindings here and there interrupted by a newer volume's garish dust jacket. It was hard to break the habit of looking, Hilary had trained me well.

My breath caught as my eye stopped on a tall blue book enclosed in a slipcase of the same hue. *Impossible!* The only other copy I'd ever seen was in the now nonexistent reading room of the old Lambs club. I practically leaped on it, looked for the price, couldn't find any. I carried it up front, keeping an aisle between me and Hilary.

"Ah-*hah*," Bannister said, his face wreathed in smiles

when he saw my selection. "A man of rarefied tastes! There's a wonderful story that goes with this volume. For twenty years—"

"Shh," I hushed him, "tell me it another time, I want to make this a surprise. How much?"

He adopted my conspiratorial whisper. "I'll give it to you for cost. Sixty dollars."

"Thanks . . . but I don't have that much money with me. Will you put it aside?"

Pressing it into my hands, Bannister said, "Go on and take it with you, lad. I trust you."

I thanked him again, but explained the book was so huge, I'd look pretty conspicuous trying to leave with it. "But I can come back tomorrow."

"Done," he said, winking, and hid it under the counter.

Farewell, my own,
  Light of my life, farewell,
For crime unknown
  I go to a dungeon cell.

When the apartment door opened, the strains of the second act octette of *H. M. S. Pinafore* reached our ears. I introduced Florence to the attorney, Hilary remaining out of sight in the hallway till Willie and I entered, then she joined the procession. The actress opened her mouth to object, but I distracted her by thrusting a dollar bill into her hand.

She frowned at the money. "What's this for?"

"To give to him," I said, indicating Willie.

"Why don't you just hand it to him yourself?"

"Because," I replied with some pique, "you're the one who needs him, and I figured I never could get you to part with a dollar of your own to ensure his discretion."

My insult earned me a nasty look and a buck for Willie. He put it in his wallet and took out the receipt he'd prepared at the bistro. As soon as Florence accepted it, the lawyer told her, "Ms. McKinley, so far as I'm concerned, you are now my client and anything I hear tonight will be regarded as a privileged communication. May I have a few words with you in private?"

"I don't intend to say a thing until my friend Lara arrives," she stated in her haughtiest manner.

"A very good idea," he agreed, nodding sagely and stroking the thing he called a beard. "You needn't speak, I'll do all the talking. Call it advice, if you wish, or perhaps rules of procedure."

She hesitated long enough for me to make a crack about her getting my dollar's worth. "And while you two are in conference," I said, "I've got a telephone call to make. Don't worry, it's local."

That was the last straw. As I'd meant it to be. Drawing herself erect—her ankle-length midnight blue dressing gown adding to her appearance of height—she told me I could use the kitchen phone. "Down that hallway. And you needn't leave a dime."

"Thanks. While I'm there, may I bring you some tea?"

"*No!*" Then she made an awkward attempt at a gracious smile. "I suppose someone else may want some."

Hilary declined, and so did I, but Willie said he wouldn't mind a scotch. A bit nervy, perhaps, but then he was on a one-buck retainer.

Looking like she might have a stroke any minute, Scrooge McKinley said, "I'm not sure I have any in the kitchen."

"Oh, as long as I'm there," I volunteered helpfully, "I'll try to find some."

"*Thank* you," she euphemized.

> *Hold! Ere upon your loss*
> *You lay much stress,*
> *A long-concealèd crime*
> *I would confess.*

As Buttercup sang her dire secret to the assembled Pinafore cast, I went to the kitchen, which was closer to the living room than my first visit led me to believe. As I entered, Florence's tubby tawny cat, Rathbone, sleepily gazed at me through half-shut eyelids. He lay comfortably ensconced in a straw basket next to the gas range, swathed in a downy blanket, and with a pillow yet.

I dialed Fat Lou's home number and gave him a down payment. He took the information without asking questions—he was on his own time. The call took us less than a minute.

Hanging up the phone, I checked the drawers and cabinet doors till I found the McKinley liquor stock. I almost burst out laughing. One shelf was crammed full of innumerable tiny flasks of every imaginable variety of whisky, cordial and liqueur, all of them miniatures.

I removed a pair of Johnny Walker Blacks, poured them over ice and brought the drink to Willie. He was standing by the picture window overlooking the river promenade talking in a low voice to Florence. I gave him the glass and joined Hilary by the aquarium.

"Housekeeping is hardly her strong suit," she said beneath her breath.

The room was the same as I saw it the night before: tables groaning under piles of scripts, sheet music and dust; the same recording paraphernalia atop the FM/phono compact. The cassette in the compartment whirled the finale of the G&S operetta to its joyous conclusion.

"Sounds like an old recording," I remarked.

"It is," Hilary nodded. "I've got it. They transferred a 1930 performance from 78s to tape. It's back to back with an even older *Trial By Jury*."

The last mock-Wagnerian *motif* sounded and in the silence that followed, the burbling of the air pump in the fish tank seemed surprisingly loud. Willie's voice momentarily stood out in the hush, but he quickly adjusted his volume, and then more music played, a piano solo, something by Gottschalk.

There was a curious frown on Hilary's face, but before

I could comment, the doorbell rang. Florence left the room and returned presently with Lara, who immediately crossed to me, apologizing for being late. But when she was a few feet away, she stopped talking and came to a halt.

"Hello, Lainie," Hilary said.

The two cousins stared at one another like mirror images, then Lara gazed at me wide-eyed, lips half-parted in an unspoken question. A second of silence, and she turned away.

Florence stopped the tape before the end and sat next to Willie on the couch. Their backs were to Hilary, who remained standing by the aquarium. Lara chose the same chair as the night before, the one opposite the sofa.

Facing the group on my feet, I had Hilary straight ahead on the other side of the couch and Lara on my right. Their stares were the legs of an obtuse angle with me at the apex, like a moth double-pinned to a specimen board.

I made an effort to ignore them and concentrate on Florence McKinley. "I'm going to construct a scenario, and you're the star. I'm taking a calculated risk doing this, and I don't expect you to appreciate it, either."

I paused, waiting for her to comment, but she just glared at me with lips pressed into a thin, grim line, evidently following Willie's advice not to speak.

"Lara," I began, "brought me here last night because you claimed someone was trying to blame Ed Niven's death on you. I checked and found out you were extremely jealous of any woman Niven so much as smiled at —and according to at least one witness, he smiled at quite a few of them. You probably had Kit Yerby fired for that reason."

She opened her mouth, then remembered and closed it again.

I went on. "It didn't take much effort on my part to discover you really called me here as a tool to get at Joanne Carpenter. It's true, of course, that she lives near WBS and has no alibi for Saturday, but then, neither do you. And in my opinion, Joanne never could have hurt him."

I phrased it deliberately to rile her, and it worked. Angrily, she began, "And you think that I have the capacity to—" But she stopped herself at a glance from Willie. A vein throbbed in her temple.

I continued. "I can't prove that you put the alcohol in Joanne's 'medicine,' but you were quick to suggest that she did it herself to further implicate you. Unfortunately, the argument cuts either way. Lacking evidence, I have to call it a stalemate."

Florence sniffed disdainfully. "Your incompetence is not my fault."

Ignoring the taunt, I said, "Hitting Ames with his Emmy showed a total lack of caution. Joanne was in the hospital when it happened, sleeping off her attack. And even if she'd been at WBS, she wouldn't have had any idea what was going on between Ames and Tommy Franklin."

"Wait a minute," the actress fumed. "I told you that I have the contractual right to review every new 'Bible'—"

Willie sternly silenced her. No wonder; she'd just made a damaging admission. Though Lara already told me she'd mentioned Franklin's proposed—and missing—'Bible' to her friend, the news from Florence's own lips was a time-saver for Fat Lou, and how he loved time-savers.

"You have the right to see an officially approved storyline," I said, "but we're not talking about that yet, are we? I assume Ames intended to tell Tommy to rewrite his little stinger to make the actual method of easing you off the show less obvious. Maybe a little vacation for Martha? Or a debilitating stroke? WBS thinks the ratings eventually will improve if Ames gets rid of you. He might even think it worth the expense to pay your salary and keep you off screen till you agree to a settlement. Maybe—"

"Gene," Willie interrupted, "can we stick to the main point?"

"Okay. You mean Niven's death. Florence lied to me and Lara about finding his clothing in her dressing room Monday morning. It was a clumsy fabrication to begin with, and now I've learned the police recovered the missing garments over the weekend."

"Where?" Florence demanded.

"I suspect you already know. All right, I said I'd outline a scenario. Here it is. Niven wanted to break it off with you. You got him to meet you on some pretext Saturday on the top floor of WBS. You entered by the side door. So did he. You met in the sleeping alcove behind Umberto's hairstyling room. You argued. Something happened, I don't know what exactly, either you hit him or he fell and struck his head. Anyway, I think that's the way Niven really died. You panicked and undressed him, carried him to the edge of the roof and let him fall, probably figuring the original wound would be eradicated on impact. They found tar on his feet, so it's my guess it got on your shoes, too, and you had to clean it off with the newspaper on the snack room table. There was a scrap of it left over."

"Gene," the lawyer interrupted, "do you have *any* hard evidence?"

"That's for you to judge. Umberto complained because one of the cots was rumpled, and its pillow missing. Somebody also stole a rather large quantity of collodion."

"And what's that?" he asked.

"A liquid containing ether. It's used in creating fake scars and things like that on TV. Highly flammable."

"What are you suggesting?"

"Add it up, Willie. Head wounds mean a lot of blood. If the falling-off-the-roof story was going to stick, she couldn't leave a bloody pillow behind. I think she doused it with the collodion. I checked, it only comes in two-ounce bottles, so she probably figured she'd need a lot of it."

"Wouldn't she have burnt his clothes as long as she was at it? For that matter, why undress him at all?"

"To shift guilt to Joanne by planting the evidence in her dressing room. Which is seldom locked. And that's where the clothing was found."

"See, I *knew* it!" Florence said, but not with much conviction. Her nerve was faltering.

"Of course you knew it," I said. "You described for me the exact list of garments the police have at this moment. What's worse, you even mentioned his bloody shirt. Now tell me, if Niven really fell off the roof naked, how could he bleed on his shirt?"

The actress was starting to look her age, and more. Her forehead and the corners of her eyes seemed more wrinkled. "Why?" she pleaded in a hoarse voice, "why are you doing this to me?"

It annoyed me more than her earlier arrogance. "You don't even know what I *am* doing. Tomorrow I have to tell the police what I think. I'm emptying the bag tonight so Willie can help you prepare some kind of defense. I'm not doing it for you, though. I don't like people who try to use me. This is a favor to Lara, because you're her friend." I paused, skewered on the cousins' unwavering stares, feeling thoroughly rotten.

"Gene," Willie asked, "is that the whole lot?"

"No. Remember the call I made before Lara got here?"

"Yes."

"It was to Inspector Betterman. I told him to pick up an old man named Woody as a potential witness. Woody just got fired from WBS as a security guard. He—"

"All right, *all right!*" Florence suddenly shrieked, clapping her hands to her ears. "No more! Not now! *Please!*"

Willie couldn't quiet her. Giving me a barbed glance, Lara waved him away and said, "Why don't the three of you go out and wait in the entryway?"

As we did as she asked, she tried to put her arms around her friend, but Florence pushed her away.

"You brought that man here in the first place," she accused Lara. "*You* did this to me! Don't think you won't suffer—"

There was more of it, but I tried to ignore it.

Several minutes later, Lara joined us. Her face looked white and drawn.

"She's a little calmer now. Not much, though. I'm going to bring her some Valium, then I suggest we all go home."

Willie and I began to protest.

"She's not going to run away," Lara said. "Look, just leave her alone for tonight, all right?"

"*Then* what?" I asked.

"Tomorrow she promises to confess everything."

Abel Harrison had dropped off Lara at Florence's, so the four of us walked silently back to my car. The weather was beginning to turn muggy.

The cousins got into the back seat and Willie rode up front with me. Neither Hilary nor Lara spoke, but Willie insisted I explain the significance of Woody in my scenario.

"He was another calculated risk on my part," I said. "I wanted to make sure, though, that Lou picked him up before I mentioned him to Florence, just in case I was right and she tried something desperate. Judging from the way she reacted, I'd say my hunch about him is accurate."

"But how does he fit in?" the attorney asked.

"They fired him the other day for saying something stupid concerning WBS security on the newscast about Niven. But when I saw him at the studio today, he seemed awfully jaunty. Not to mention very expensively dressed. Brand-new threads."

"So?"

"I also spotted him waiting on a park bench last night on the pedestrian walk behind Florence's apartment, looking up at her windows. Maybe he was waiting for her to blink the lights as a signal that Lara and I were gone?"

"Hmm." Willie mulled it over. "Was he on duty when Niven fell?"

"Yes."

"You're suggesting blackmail. You think this Woody saw her at WBS Saturday?"

"That's for Fat Lou to find out," I said, steering into the bridge lane.

After dropping Willie off on Twenty-third Street, I headed west to Eleventh and started uptown, wondering whether either woman in the back seat intended to speak to me again.

Lara did. "I'd like to be driven directly home."

When I pulled up in front of her building, Lara's doorman recognized her and hurried over to let her out of the car. She told Hilary good night, but I only got a brusque nod. I watched her disappear into her lobby.

"Were you planning to stay with her this evening?" Hilary asked with uncharacteristic gentleness.

I shrugged. "My things are up there."

A long silence before Hilary spoke again. "Gene . . . you never took all your clothes . . ."

It took me a second to comprehend.

"Hilary, are you saying I can spend the night at your place?"

"It's just that you look too worn out to drive back to Philly. I mean, it's only one night, and your room's empty."

I accepted with some misgivings.

I parked in the garage on Eighty-seventh Street where Hilary keeps her VW. She let me in and offered me tea or brandy before bedtime. It wasn't very late, but she said she had an early business appointment.

"I'm pretty tired, Hilary. Would you mind if I had tea in my old room?"

"Not at all. I'll bring it to you."

It was strange entering my old quarters. The fact that Harry Whelan occupied them for six months didn't matter. The place still felt like mine. I checked the closet and found a few shirts and one suit that belonged to me. They were too heavy for the season, but it'd be better than wearing the same things I'd had on for two days. I looked in the bureau and found underwear and socks. I couldn't remember leaving any, but they were my size, so I was grateful. A quick shower, and I got in bed.

A rap on the door. I bade Hilary enter.

She brought me a cup of gunpowder tea, another favorite of mine. Putting it on the nightstand by the headboard, she sat on the edge of the bed, staring into her hands resting lifelessly in her lap. I thanked her for the tea, but didn't take it yet. I wanted to hear what she evidently had on her mind.

It took her a while to say it. "I don't blame you, Gene, for liking Lainie."

"Does it make any difference whether I do or not? When Harry left, you certainly didn't break any records to bring me back."

She gave me a hard look, and for a second, I thought I was due for one of her verbal rapier thrusts. But she wrestled with it and locked it away.

Turning from me gave me a chance to gaze at Hilary for a while. I don't remember when she looked lovelier. Her blond hair, loose and flowing—the way I'd always preferred it—framed the perfect oval of her face. Her eyes might have shamed a sapphire, and she wore a pale blue robe over matching pajamas, an ensemble I'd given her last year. It reminded me her birthday was coming soon.

She turned back and I lowered my eyes. "Gene," she asked quietly, "what went wrong with us?"

"Us, I suppose."

"Was it Washington?"

"No. That was only symptomatic. Anyway, Harry told me nothing happened there."

"He lied."

I turned aside for my teacup, needing some activity to mask my feelings. It upset me that it still mattered.

"I was angry at you, angry at your becoming so important to me, Gene. I wanted Harry to exorcise you. Only he couldn't."

I said nothing. I took a sip of tea and did not speak.

The silence grew longer and longer. Hilary finally broke it. "Damn it, Gene, talk to me!"

"What do you expect me to say?"

"*Any*thing!"

I put down the teacup. "Hilary, what you've told me is none of my business."

She stiffened. Her lips drew into an angry line, but still she didn't lash back. Instead, she rose from the bed and started out, stopping at the door.

"I'm sorry I disturbed you," Hilary said softly, and left.

Without her, the room grew cold.

Next morning when I woke, I found a note on my nightstand.

Gene, I'm sorry about last night. We were both tired and upset. Lainie called late, but you were sound asleep. She's not working today and hopes you'll come over early. If you need me, I'll be back around five. If you're short of cash, there's about $150 in the office safe. You know the combination.

As a matter of fact, I *was* short and didn't have my checkbook with me. I borrowed one hundred dollars, left an IOU, and promised myself I'd pay her back as soon as I got home.

I got dressed and went outside. Rain brought no overnight relief. Though West End Avenue was pockmarked with puddles, the sun blazed mercilessly and, by the time I got to Lara's penthouse, the heavy clothes I'd donned were moist with perspiration.

Lara opened her door and rushed into my arms.

"Gene, I'm sorry, I'm sorry, forgive me!"

She clung to me and I felt the sweet warmth of her flesh. Sensibly clad in lightweight halter and pastel-colored shorts, she wore a subtle flush of rouge on her cheeks and just enough eye shadow to draw me into their depths. Though she looked like she'd been crying, she was more glamorous now than ever she'd been on "Riverday."

I put my arms around her and we kissed.

In the dim softness of her bedroom I cradled her in my arms and stared at the amber glow of the digital clock.

10:15 A.M. I wanted to ask about Abel, but it was the wrong time for it, and anyway, I was starting to get antsy about calling Lou Betterman. I told Lara, and she nodded sadly.

"All right," she said. "But let me phone Flo first."

"Isn't she at work?"

"No. Mack told us they'd be shooting around the Jennett family today. It's all sideplots till Joanne returns tomorrow."

I lay back against the pillows while Lara went into the other room to call Florence. She was only gone a short time when she reentered the bedroom, clearly distressed.

"Lara, what's wrong?"

"It's Florence, she sounds strange."

"Strange *how?*"

"Drugged."

"Probably the Valium. What did she say?"

"That she was going to clean up the mess she made. Then she hung up on me."

My backbone went icy. Leaping out of bed, I ran to the living room. "What's her number?"

"It's by the phone."

There was a memo book; I flipped to the "M" page, found Florence's name and dialed. It rang three times before I heard it being picked up.

"Who is this? Lara?" Florence's voice was indeed thick and curiously flat.

I identified myself. A sharp intake of breath on the other end, followed by a longish pause which I waited out.

"Leave me alone," her voice finally murmured. "You can't hurt me any more." A loud noise, as if the phone fell to the floor. I yelled her name, there was a kind of scrabbling on the other end, then a click and the line went dead.

"Come on," I told Lara, slamming down the receiver and dashing for the bedroom and my clothes. "We've got to get over there *fast!*"

In any other city, I would've gotten ten tickets for the way I drove, but in New York, it hardly mattered. I pulled up across the street from Florence's home, stopping next to a No Parking sign, the only empty space.

Upstairs, Lara began to unlock the apartment, but I stopped her. "Wait! Leave the key in the door and get back!"

"Gene, she's *my* friend!"

"Damn it," I shouted, "go down the hall and *wait!*"

She reluctantly obeyed. I turned the key the rest of the way, then, holding a handkerchief over my nose and mouth, very gently turned the knob and pushed in the door.

The smell of gas was overwhelming.

Taking a deep breath, I passed cautiously through the hall and into the living room. Grabbing the first heavy object I could lay my hand on, I hurled it through the picture window, part of which shattered. Luckily, the house is set back a distance from the promenade; there was little danger of the fragments injuring someone below. Gasping for air, I seized a chair and swung it repeatedly against the window, widening the ragged aperture.

In the rush of fresh air, I turned and saw Florence seated in a nearby armchair, white and stiff. I tried to find a pulse or heartbeat, but failed. Her skin felt as waxy as it looked, and her limbs were rigid.

Sucking in as much fresh air as my lungs could hold, I started towards the kitchen.

The oven and all four burners were on. The pilot light was out. I turned everything off and stood by the range staring stupidly, trying to clear my head. My eyes were tearing and my knees felt weak.

"*Gene!*"

Lara swayed in the kitchen archway gasping for breath, face pale with terror. I stumbled to her and the two of us lurched down the hall like drunkards. She staggered through the front entrance first, and I crawled the last few feet, collapsing in a heap outside.

After we felt better and the fresh air had a chance to circulate, we cautiously returned to the apartment. I asked Lara to call the police while I went back to the living room.

Now that I could look around without squinting, I saw the typewritten note taped to the aquarium. I walked over and almost started the air pump, but then stopped myself; I didn't know for a fact that all the gas was gone, and the switch might spark.

I read Florence's note without removing it from the glass.

> *I killed Ed Niven out of jealousy in the manner described last night before three witnesses. I attempted to implicate Joanne Carpenter by planting his clothes in her dressing room. Later I put alcohol into prop medicine I knew she would swallow during taping. I struck Joseph T. Ames when he caught me reading certain private papers in his office.*
>
> *I cannot live with this disgrace.*

Florence was in the armchair near the aquarium, the same she'd occupied Monday night when Lara helped her relax before bedtime by plumping up the pillows, bringing her a ton of Valium and tuning in WQXR. My eyes automatically drifted to her sound system, then back again to the dead woman.

I felt a hard knot in my stomach. What was taking Lara so long? Had I sent her into the kitchen too soon? Maybe the gas hadn't all cleared. Going down the hall, I looked in, but she wasn't there. I stopped for a moment, trying to quiet the growing tightness inside. I turned and hurried further down the corridor.

I found Lara just hanging up the phone in a small blue bedchamber, the first neat room I'd seen in the apartment. It was warm and cheery with a fluffy carpet and canopied bed that was all lace hangings and puffed pillows. The dresser was covered with Irish linen held in place by a framed portrait of Florence arm in arm with a man I knew was Ed Niven from the picture I'd seen in the newspaper. A polished mahogany night table held the extension phone and message unit, while underneath, its shelves were full of scrapbooks bulging and trailing edges and faded brown corners of tattered newspaper and magazine clippings, the last scraps of a life that started when a nine-year-old girl did a specialty dance on the Ted Mack Amateur Hour.

"The ambulance will be here any minute," Lara said.

"Good. Why don't you wait outside for it? It's healthier."

"How about you?"

"I'd better call Lou first."

When she was gone, I rang up the inspector and gave him a fast précis of the past twelve or thirteen hours and promised I'd stick around till he got there.

Then I went back to the living room, pulled the microphone out of the sound system and pried the *H. M. S. Pinafore* cassette from Florence's stiff fingers.

I put it in my pocket and went downstairs.

Since there was absolutely nothing else Lara could do, and she had her next day's script to learn, I prevailed upon Fat Lou to let her go. There was no chance of getting away myself, so I submitted to a barrage of questions, which I handled pretty well, glossing over ambiguities with qualifiers like "in my opinion" and "to the best of my knowledge." Hanging around actors a few days honed my technique.

Betterman eventually released me, and I trudged over to Montague Street, opening the buttons of my shirt as I went. My car was in a garage near the bistro where Hilary, Willie and I had passed a pleasant half-hour the night before; I'd moved it after the emergency squad arrived and before Lou showed up.

As I passed the bistro, a few thoughts occurred to me. I went inside. The place was cool and nearly empty. I stepped up to the bar, ordered a double Bushmill's, downed it and then requested a Beck's. I took bottle and glass over to the wall telephone.

I had no luck at Polyclinic, but Micki gave me Joanne's private number without too much fuss. I got the actress in on the first ring.

After we were through talking, I called Jess Brass' office and made an appointment to see her in an hour. Then I returned to the bar and ordered a refill.

"Of which?" the bartender asked. "The Bush or the beer?"

"Both."

It was a program I intended to pick up again after I saw the columnist.

When Hilary entered her lobby shortly after five o'clock, she found me sprawled on the green leather sofa waiting for her.

"Left my car in Brooklyn Heights," I said, carefully pronouncing each syllable.

"I should *hope* you didn't drive in that condition. What's wrong with you? Never mind, tell me inside after you've had some coffee."

"No, no," I said, ponderously shaking my head, "haven't you heard? Coffee's bad for the pancreas."

"I'd suggest you worry about your liver first. Are you able to stand?"

"For *what?*"

She sighed. "All right, brightness, put your arm around me. I'll help you."

I think I said something stupid then, me or someone else hiding inside, but damned if I remember what. All I can clearly recall is Hilary smiling at me with a kind of curious sadness, and then the next thing I knew, she had her door open and I was slouching in her office, sitting in my old chair slopping black coffee all over my chin.

Twenty-five minutes later, give or take. Lots of caffeine followed by aspirin. Hilary never lost her patience, raised her voice or blamed me, but once I was coherent again, she pulled her desk chair close to mine.

"All right, Gene, what's the matter? I never saw you like this before."

"Florence McKinley's dead."

"Oh, *no!*"

"Yes. I phoned her this morning from Lara's, didn't like what I heard, rushed over there and found Florence in front of her fish tank with the gas on."

"We never should have left her alone last night."

"No. But Lara insisted—"

The doorbell rang. Hilary answered the summons and let in her cousin. Lara was in lightweight gray slacks and blouse and had her hair pinned in a net. She was carrying a script. When she saw me, her eyes widened.

"Gene, I had no idea where you got to. I thought you would've called by now."

"Well, I asked Hilary to invite you over. I've got something I thought you'd want to hear." I fished in my pockets till I found the *H. M. S. Pinafore* cassette, the second of a set of two. One side contained the last half of the second act from the "Bell Trio" to the Finale, while the other held a complete performance (1927 D'Oyly Carte) of *Trial By Jury*. I handed it to Hilary and asked her to bring out her tape recorder and put on Side A.

Lara looked dubious. "Gene, I don't have much time. I've got lines to learn for—"

"Trust me," I interrupted. "There might be something worth hearing besides Gilbert and Sullivan. I found this tape clutched in Florence's hand this morning."

The cousins stared at me, surprised and shocked. "Lou let you take this with you?" Hilary asked skeptically.

"Nope. He doesn't know it exists." I pointed to the label. "Hilary, note the timings."

She held it up and read, "Side B, *Trial By Jury*, thirty minutes thirty seconds. Side A, *Pinafore* Act II Conclusion, nineteen minutes and nine seconds. Hmm. Roughly eleven minutes of blank runoff at the end of Side A."

"So what?" Lara asked.

"So," said Hilary, immediately on my wavelength, "we

all know Florence McKinley was a penny pincher. I suppose she couldn't stand the notion of wasting eleven whole minutes of tape. In fact, the thought crossed my mind last night when—"

"Look, this is silly," Lara broke in. "You can't record on a commercial cassette. They're manufactured so they won't work that way on a home machine. I know, I tried it once."

"Lainie, look at *this* one." Hilary pointed to a pair of thin strips of adhesive pasted over the two holes on the ends of the top edge of the cassette. "That's all it takes. The holes are punched by the manufacturer to prevent accidental taping over of their album on home machines. But if you cover the apertures with Scotch tape, you can then use the empty footage that you sometimes find at the end of commercial reels. As a matter of fact, Lainie, I noticed that Florence kept a roll of tape on the dust cover of her phonograph, right next to an FM program guide."

"Uh-huh," I nodded, "so did I."

Hilary put down the cassette and left the room to get her recorder. While she was gone, Lara hovered over her cousin's desk, examining the tape. After a moment, she turned to me.

"Gene, maybe Flo had some music playing at the end. She might've just taken this out of the recorder and—"

"No." I shook my head. "She was definitely making a voice recording. When I found her body, I noticed a microphone plugged into her sound system. It wasn't there last night when we left."

Lara might've asked me something else, but Hilary returned with her portable cassette machine and put Side A of the tape in it. Lara took the black leatherette lounge seat near Hilary's desk and watched her cousin press fast forward, monitor, fast forward, monitor, eventually bringing the recording down to speed at the recitative preceding Buttercup's penultimate song.

"Close enough," said Hilary. "Let's listen."

> *Hold! Ere upon your loss*
> *You lay much stress,*
> *A long-concealèd crime*
> *I would confess.*

Pinafore never had a grimmer audience. The three of us sat sober-faced through the literal last Hurrahs of the jolly operetta. A long ensuing silence—then we again heard the solo piano piece by Gottschalk.

"*Le Bananier,*" Hilary said. "It surprised me last night when it began to play. Florence didn't change the cassette, yet instead of G&S, Gottschalk suddenly emerged from the speakers. That made about as much sense as coupling a Bach toccata to a Loretta Lynn disc, so I figured Florence probably was in the habit of using segments of blank tape on her commercial albums to record music off FM."

The piano solo ended. Another pause. I glanced at Lara, but saw nothing more in her face than casual interest. Hilary, however, seemed unusually intent. We waited out the silence. Suddenly, we heard the unmistakable voice of Florence McKinley.

MEMO TO MR. WILLARD FROST

MOST OF WHAT LARA'S FRIEND SAID WAS TRUE. ED CALLED, SAID WE NEEDED TO TALK SATURDAY. HE WAS WORKING UP THE NEW "BIBLE," SO WE MET FOR LUNCH NEAR THE STUDIO. HE TOLD ME HE INTENDED TO BREAK OFF WITH ME. HE SAID THERE WAS ANOTHER WOMAN. OF COURSE I GREW UPSET, SO HE TOOK ME OUT OF THE RESTAURANT BECAUSE HE NEVER COULD ABIDE PUBLIC SCENES. WE WENT TO WBS, BUT THE GUARD WAS ON HIS

ROUNDS AND THE LOBBY ACCESS DOOR WAS LOCKED, SO
WE TRIED THE OUTSIDE FIRE EXIT AND FOUND IT OPEN.
WE AVOIDED ED'S OFFICE—TOO NEAR THE NEWSROOM—
AND ANYWAY, WE'VE OFTEN GONE TO THE TOP FLOOR
SLEEPING ALCOVE TO BE ALONE.

WE ARGUED. HE TOLD ME I WAS CONDUCTING A VEN-
DETTA AGAINST JOANNE CARPENTER, WHICH TOLD ME
WHO WAS BEHIND IT ALL. I CRIED. ED NEVER COULD
STAND A WOMAN'S TEARS. HE DID HIS BEST TO COMFORT
ME, AND WE ENDED UP MAKING LOVE, BUT AFTERWARDS
. . . NEVER MIND. HE INSULTED ME. OUT OF ANGER, I
PUSHED HIM AWAY FROM ME. THAT'S WHEN HE LOST
HIS BALANCE, FELL AND HIT HIS HEAD.

A longish silence. Her breath sighed unnaturally loud
over the speaker. When she resumed, her voice grew in-
creasingly languid.

IT WAS AN ACCIDENT, BUT I PANICKED. YOU HEARD
ESSENTIALLY WHAT HAPPENED TONIGHT FROM LARA'S
FRIEND. I TOOK THE PILLOW TO THE BASEMENT TO BURN
IT. ON THE WAY BACK UP, OLD WOODY SAW ME. I ASKED
HIM NOT TO MENTION I WAS THERE AND GAVE HIM A
FEW DOLLARS. BUT HE CALLED ME ON SUNDAY AND SAID
HE'D BEEN FIRED, SO I'D BETTER HELP HIM OUT. I TRIED
TO PUT HIM OFF, BUT HE INSISTED ON SEEING ME MON-
DAY NIGHT AFTER LARA AND GENE LEFT. I WAS LATE TO
WORK THE NEXT MORNING BECAUSE I HAD TO STOP AT
THE BANK AND MAKE A LARGE WITHDRAWAL WHICH
WOODY PICKED UP LATER THAT MORNING AT WBS. AND
THAT'S—

Click. The cassette ran out of tape and stopped.
Lara exhaled audibly. "She never finished."
I shrugged. "I suspect she was pretty close to done.
Wouldn't you say so, Hilary?"

"I don't know. She didn't have time to mention either Joanne's poisoning or Ames' clubbing."

"Hilary, come off it, don't you know what she would have said?"

"No, I don't." She gazed at me oddly. "Gene, why did you remove this tape? Won't Lou need it?"

"No. I took care of all that. Let's not get sidetracked. On Sunday, you and Lara came to my place in Philly. What was going on then between the two of you?"

The cousins exchanged glances. Hilary's fingers tapped a rapid tattoo on her desk top. "I don't know what you're talking about, Gene."

"Bullshit. The lady who solved the Third Murderer problem in *Macbeth* can't comprehend the language of a mere male?"

"Who in hell do you think you're talking to?" Hilary tried to fix me with a steely stare, but for once couldn't bring it off. She rose and bought a little time by fussing with the cassette, popping it out of her portable and slapping it on her desk. Lara's attention was entirely focused on her cousin. Finally, Hilary sat back down and addressed me in a cool, flat tone of voice. "All right, just out of curiosity, what do you think you noticed between me and Lara?"

"At the time, nothing I could put a name to. Earlier, when that bitch Jess Brass showed Lara the news of Niven's death, maybe I should've picked up on the effect, but I didn't. Later on, though, at my apartment, I sensed some kind of subtext running between the two of you. Lara used my phone to talk with Florence in New York. After the call was over, Lara said Florence believed someone was trying to set herself up to take the blame for Niven falling off the roof. When you heard that, you acted absolutely stunned. Why?"

"No theories?"

"Obviously yes, and you know it, but I'd prefer you to say it."

Hilary again looked at Lara. For the duration of a ten-second hour, no one spoke. Hilary's fingers began to drum the arm of her chair, but she clenched her fist and dropped it to her lap. "I'm sorry, Gene, there's nothing I can tell you."

I sighed. "All right, then I'll do the talking. Joanne Carpenter was not the other woman who came between Florence and Niven. It was Lara." I turned to her to stifle the protest already on her lips. "Don't bother with another of your performances. You've lost your audience." Back to Hilary. "My guess is that your cousin dated Abel Harrison partly for the professional contacts he has on both coasts, but mainly as a convenient smoke screen for her romance with Niven. Lara was one of the few women Florence didn't consider a threat, presumably because she was convinced that Lara was already answered for."

"When did you come up with this notion?" Hilary asked.

"Today. Lots of little things fell into place. How Lara reacted to the news of Niven's death. Your behavior with her at my apartment. The casual things I heard Lara say that revealed she knew a hell of a lot about how Niven worked and thought. The men's toiletries in her bathroom cabinet."

"All right, Gene," Hilary said, her lips and eyebrows both drawn down, "I guess there's no point in pretending I don't know what you're talking about—"

"*Hilary!*"

"Lainie, for God's sake, he *knows*. Give the man credit for some brains, and level with him for once!" Hilary faced me. "Lainie and Ed kept their relationship quiet for fear that Florence would try to wreck Lainie's career. But

then the situation . . . the situation grew more complicated. Last weekend, while Lainie and I were out of
town attending soap festivals, Ed promised he'd break off
with Florence. Saturday, while we were on the road, he
planned to meet her near the studio. Late that day, my
cousin began to worry when Ed didn't call back to say
what happened. She phoned his apartment and office, but
he wasn't either place. She grew afraid he'd had a change
of heart and was spending the weekend with Florence.
We didn't get any answers till that vulture showed the
story to Lainie, and you saw how she almost went into
shock.

"When I read about his death, I immediately suspected
Florence of killing him in a jealous rage. Sunday, at your
place in Philly, I acted strange because Florence asked
my cousin to come see her in Brooklyn Heights. I thought
she was trying to lure 'the other woman' into a trap.
That's why I insisted on going along, though as it turned
out, that poor neurotic fool had no idea who 'the other
woman' was. Or at least, that's what Lainie said." Hilary
swiveled in her chair. "Why didn't you tell me Florence
suspected Joanne?"

"I didn't see any reason to," Lara replied. "Why mention something that isn't true?"

Considering the source, I nearly laughed. Hilary began
to berate Lara for using me to get over her grief for
Niven, but for once she was off the mark, and I stopped
her.

"Lara used me, all right, Hilary, but not the way you
think."

"What do you mean?"

"Look, Hilary, while you were waiting in Florence's
hallway, what do you think she was really telling Lara?
The truth? Or some lie that Lara instantly saw through

because she already knew Flo met Niven Saturday? I'd guess the latter, how about you?"

"Gene, what are you driving at?"

"Flo was a lousy liar, I have personal knowledge of that fact. Her story must've been so feeble that I suppose Lara figured it'd be seen through immediately by the police. Except that didn't happen. That's probably when Lara decided to go after Florence herself, with me as her principal tool."

"That's absolute nonsense!" Lara exclaimed.

"*Is* it? Tell me this, dear Cousin Lainie—'who could always get away with things without being caught or scolded'—do you intend to have an abortion?"

Lara stiffened.

"Well," I said, "isn't that what Hilary meant just now by saying the situation got 'more complicated'? I hope you weren't counting on me to make you an honest woman."

Lara looked as if I'd punched her. I had to keep reminding myself what an actress she was, or I couldn't've continued. I faced Hilary again. She was as pale as her cousin. "I imagine Lara planted the idea in Florence's head of hiring me to track down evidence of Joanne's guilt. Of course, Flo pretended my job was just to clear her of suspicion in Niven's death, but it didn't take long to surmise what she actually wanted me to do. Yet my real assignment—the one Lara scripted for me—was to nail Florence. To make it easier, she slipped Joanne a dose of Antabuse."

Lara stood up. "I don't have to stay and listen to this."

I shrugged. "Suit yourself. But if you go, you'll just have to wonder what else I said to Hilary."

Lara sat down.

"Florence's hatred for Joanne," I resumed, "was well

THE SOAP OPERA SLAUGHTERS

known at 'Riverday.' So was her habit of going off by herself to prepare for upcoming scenes. All anyone had to do was look at a taping schedule and consult a floor plan of the day's shooting to see that Florence could've been near the hospital set unobserved before Joanne got sick."

"Gene," Hilary said, holding up a hand for silence, "maybe you'd better not tell me anything else. Unless you're prepared to back up what you're saying."

I shook my head. "I don't have anything that'll hold up in court. But call Joanne and ask her about the lunch she and Lara had on Monday."

"Why?"

"Because when *I* phoned her earlier today, Joanne said she remembered how Lara steered the conversation around to the subject of illnesses. She seemed especially interested in finding out whether Joanne ever had any serious physical problems. Such as heart trouble."

"For God's sake," Lara objected, "since when is personal health a taboo topic? What in hell does this prove?"

Hilary answered it. "It suggests you might've done homework on the contraindications of Antabuse and wanted to make sure Joanne wouldn't be in any genuine danger."

"Hilary, you're not starting to believe him?"

I said, "When I jumped in front of the cameras because Joanne looked ill, Lara was right behind me, urging that we take Joanne straight to Polyclinic. Manny the druggist advised the same thing on the phone. You don't treat an Antabuse reaction solely with first aid."

"And then," Hilary murmured, half to herself, "there's the matter of one Joseph T. Ames."

"Yes." I nodded. "Besides you and me and Micki Lipscomb, the only other person directly to hear about Tommy Franklin's proposed 'Bible' was Lara—and she immediately told Florence. Franklin intimated he thought he'd come up with a way to write the part of Mother Jennett out of 'Riverday.' Lara must've figured the suspicion naturally would fall on Florence if Franklin's pages disappeared from Ames' desk.

"My guess is that Ames came in unexpectedly and Lara had no choice but to hit him so she wouldn't be discovered going through his things. In a way, it was my fault. Lara heard me say the poisoning was at a stalemate, there didn't seem to be any way to pin it either on Florence or Joanne herself. So Lara tried another ploy, one that culminated in Ames getting his head bashed."

That was all I had to say. I waited for one or the other cousin to move or talk or do something, but neither one did, so after a long time, I got to my feet.

"I'm feeling marginally better," I told Hilary. "I'm going to splurge on a taxi to 'the Heights' and get my car."

"What about Lara?"

"What about her?"

"You have no real proof she did anything to Ames or Carpenter."

"I'm aware of that, Hilary."

"You also realize I'm going to ignore whatever you've said?"

"That's your privilege." I grasped the knob of the front door. "Or maybe your duty."

"Gene, what about this tape? How can I give it to Lou Betterman without landing you in trouble for removing it from Florence's apartment?"

"You can't. Better let me have it back."

Hilary handed me the cassette. "Maybe," she suggested, "you can mail it to him anonymously."

"That's a possibility," I agreed. "Or I might just burn the damned thing." I turned to Lara, steeling myself against the artful vulnerability she was projecting. "Which do you suggest, 'Cousin Lainie'?"

I left before she answered.

But as I expected, Lara caught up with me in the lobby.

"Gene," she began, "you can't really believe there was nothing more between us than—"

"Than what? Can you even find a name for it? Do you really want to? The only thing I believe is that you took me to bed to gain my total cooperation and trust."

"How can you think a woman could be that calculating?" The classic feminine Innocence Wronged act, and she was very good at it. "Yes, okay, I loved Ed, and I was hurting. I turned to the nearest decent and sympathetic man. If that's what you call being used, then all right, Gene, I'm guilty. But—"

I cut her off. "But you weren't too upset to forget you had to get up early next morning for work."

"Wh-what?"

"I doublechecked. You keep your alarm clock in your bedroom. Except for Monday night, when it was in the living room where I was bunked out. Signifying you knew that's where you'd end up before morning."

A few seconds while it sank in, then I started to walk away, wondering how far I'd get before—

"Gene, don't go . . . *please!*"

Halfway to the front door was how far. I waited while she caught up with me.

"Yes, Lara? What now?"

"It . . . it doesn't have to be over, you know." She rested her fingers lightly on my arm. "Isn't there anything I can do to . . . to make things up? *Anything?*"

I was tempted to call her bluff, just to see if I could shock her, but it wasn't worth it. I shook my head. That's when Lara finally stopped acting. Stepping backward, she brought her eyes up level with mine. I saw nothing tender in them.

"How much?" All the warmth was gone from her voice.

"You can't buy it."

"Then you're going to the police?"

"That's how little you know me," I said, equally cold. "You're still Hilary's cousin." I put the cassette into her hand. "I'm not about to drop the last shovelful of dirt on her—though neither of us can prevent her from reading a newspaper or catching a telecast and drawing her own conclusions about that contradictory 'suicide note' you stuck on the front of Florence's aquarium."

Lara snapped her purse shut on the cassette. "I don't know what you're talking about."

"Not much you don't. There's no reason why Flo would've left two notes. The one we just listened to is exactly what she said it was, a memo to her lawyer, Willie Frost, nothing more." I ruefully shook my head. "I really bought the whole bit, didn't I? Dragging in Willie so Florence might get off as lightly as she could, because I thought that'd please you most. The irony must've infuriated you."

She ignored the remark. "And why," Lara asked, "would I stick up a message on the fish tank? What possible reason—"

"Come off it. You murdered Florence and you know I know it."

"For Christ's sake," she snapped, "lower your voice!" She glanced nervously about to make sure no one in the lobby was listening.

"Maybe you don't consider it murder," I conceded. "Possibly you regard it as an execution. You might be right." Possibly. I had grave doubts about Flo's ability to shove Niven hard enough to kill him. Especially when there was a sharp knife nearby, the same knife I saw resting across the top of the open peanut butter jar, its blade thickly smeared with the sticky stuff. Admittedly conjecture, but something else was a fact: Lara was Jess Brass' spy on "Riverday," and Florence knew it. It took some wrangling to verify it, but Brass finally decided to protect herself, not her source. Lara, already annoyed that Flo might get off lightly for Niven's death, suddenly was faced with her "friend" threatening her for bringing me into the case in the first place. If Flo divulged Lara's secret to the producer, Lara's career in soap opera (and possibly on TV) would be over. So after we all left Brooklyn Heights and Florence—sitting in front of her aquarium waiting for the Valium and the graceful mesmerism of the goldfish to lull her to sleep—recorded her memo to Willie, not even noticing when the tape ran out, Lara, meanwhile, affected a convenient anger at me. It enabled her to enter her building alone, wait a while, then return to Brooklyn and let herself in with her key. By then, Flo must've been perfectly catatonic and Lara could do what she wanted without fear of disturbing her. Of course, Lara couldn't risk signing the fake suicide message, but then everybody on "Riverday" was aware that Flo never willingly put her name to any piece of paper.

Lara knew I knew she did it—her need to get her hands on the cassette gave it away—but she was brazening it out, anyway, now that she had the tape safely in her purse. "I wonder," she said, "how you can possibly believe I killed Flo when you talked to her on the phone from my apartment less than an hour before we found her today?"

"It's simple forensics, Lara. If she'd really been talking to me on the phone this morning, she never would've been so stiff thirty or forty minutes later. *Rigor mortis* sets in pretty fast during hot weather, but the degree of its progress was suspicious, to say the least. On top of that, Flo's skin had a waxy, pallid appearance. Conclusion, lividity was already far advanced. That's the pooling of a dead body's blood at the lowest level gravity can draw it. The process tends to take a lot longer than half an hour.

"It took one more piece of evidence, though, to make me realize what you actually did last night. Once I saw it, the pattern fell into place . . . how you recorded the few words I thought I heard Flo say this morning." I was really talking to Flo's phone message device. Her voice was always easy to imitate. Impressionists had done it time and again on TV variety shows. "Of course, I noticed how strange and slow and flat she sounded, but I attributed that to her being drugged."

"You can't prove any of this," Lara said.

"I know I can't. It's all gone now, or at least misinterpreted. If Fat Lou did hear that cassette, he might wonder about it, but I don't think he'd come up with anything to suggest that Flo didn't turn on her stove during the night. This morning, when I sent you to her bedroom to call an ambulance, I imagine you used the opportunity to erase the message you recorded last night for my benefit."

Lara did not reply. The smart thing would've been just to stonewall me and maintain her cover, such as it was. But she had to ask it. Otherwise, it'd never allow her any peace of mind.

"Gene . . . ?"

"What?"

"You claim you noticed one more piece of—uh—alleged evidence . . . ?"

My lip curled scornfully. "I wouldn't trouble your pretty little head over it, Lara, Fat Lou wouldn't put any stock in it. But as far as I'm concerned, it's the one thing I saw that positively convinced me that Florence did not commit suicide."

"Wh-what?"

"If she'd wanted to take her own life, she could've simply OD'd on booze and pills. She never would've gassed Rathbone."

I left her standing there, went outside and hailed a cab in front of Hilary's door. When I told the driver where I was headed, he asked if he could follow the West Side Highway part of the way. I said I didn't care.

It was twilight. I'd reach "the Heights" in time to stop at The Night Owl and buy the book from Bannister. It was Percy MacKaye's *Hamlet, King of Denmark*—Hilary's Number One Want—and I planned to send it to her for her upcoming birthday.

The cabbie turned west on Seventy-ninth and the angry red rim of the dying sun stung my eyes. I felt miserable, physically and emotionally drained, and I wasn't greatly pleased with myself for the tawdry little dream I'd cherished out of loneliness. But that was all done now.

The driver said something to me in a voice as gritty as an oyster bed.

"What?" I asked him to repeat.

"I said, see that sunset?"

"Yeah—what about it?"

"They put it out for tourists," he replied. "It ain't real."

Marvin Kaye is a prolific and versatile writer of mystery and fantasy fiction. In addition to the five novels in the Hilary Quayle series (of which the best known is *Bullets for Macbeth*), he is also the author of the Marty Gold mysteries, *My Son, The Druggist* and *My Brother, The Druggist,* both published for the Crime Club. His fantasy fiction includes *The Incredible Umbrella, The Amorous Umbrella, The Possession of Immanuel Wolf,* and three novels coauthored with Parke Godwin: *The Masters of Solitude* and the forthcoming *Wintermind* and *A Cold Blue Light.* He has also written several books on magic. Mr. Kaye teaches mystery and fantasy writing at New York University and lives on New York's Upper West Side.